FARAWAY

When Laura glimpsed herself in the mirror, she hardly looked like the ballerina in the "Snowflakes" dance at last year's recital. Her nylon leotard and tights felt scratchy and twisty. She couldn't get her long hair into a nice smooth bun the way her mother always did. And, of course, her favorite other dancing Snowflake was two thousand miles away in Kansas.

Laura looked at a picture on her dresser. There were she and Molly together, all made up for the show and glittering in their white-and-silver-sequined tutus. "When are you coming home?" Laura whispered.

P.S. We'll Miss You

Yours 'Til the Meatball Bounces

2 Sweet 2 B 4-Gotten

Remember Me, When This You See

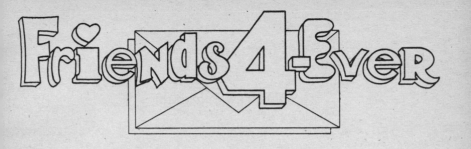

2 SWEET 2 B 4-GOTTEN

Deirdre Corey

AN
APPLE
PAPERBACK

SCHOLASTIC INC.
New York Toronto London Auckland Sydney

To Marisa Baldaccini

ISBN 0-590-42625-7

Copyright © 1990 by Fastback Press, Inc. All rights reserved. Published by Scholastic Inc. FRIENDS 4-EVER is a trademark of Scholastic Inc. APPLE PAPERBACKS is a registered trademark of Scholastic Inc.

12 11 10 9 8 7 6 5 4   0 1 2 3 4 5/9

Printed in the U.S.A.   40

First Scholastic printing, July 1990

UNLUCKY LETTER

Laura Ryder was glad that Brent Lewin was finally back in school. Brent was the tallest and widest boy in Mrs. Higgle's fourth-grade class and sat directly in front of Laura. If she positioned herself right behind his shoulders, she could have a few precious minutes away from Mrs. Higgle's hawk eyes.

Today Brent's red-and-blue rugby shirt blocked out Mrs. Higgle completely. Laura put down her pencil and sat back in her chair, pleased that she had done some extra math

pages the night before. Now she had a few minutes to doodle or close her eyes or just wait for
afternoon recess, fifteen long minutes away.

"One fourth is *smaller* than one half, Rachel!"
Mrs. Higgle said for the whole class to hear.
Rachel Garrity frantically erased her mistake as
Mrs. Higgle stood over her. "Fourths are smaller
than halves, don't you see?"

"But four is a bigger number than — " Rachel
sputtered.

"Not in fractions!" Mrs. Higgle exclaimed.

Thank goodness for Meg, Laura thought. Just
the week before on the way home from school,
Laura's best friend, Meg Milano, had shown
how Mrs. Palmer, the other fourth-grade
teacher, explained fractions. Meg took two sticks
about the same size and broke one into four
small pieces and the other into two. Right away,
Laura could see that each of the four pieces was
smaller than each of the two. The night before,
Laura zoomed ahead a few extra pages in her
math book and didn't have to worry about Mrs.
Higgle catching her in a mistake.

As the other kids struggled along, Laura
watched the big black-and-white clock over the

doorway. Twelve more minutes until she would see Meg and her other best friend, Stevie Ames. They were right across the hall, breathing the same school air, working on the same math book, and waiting for the same recess. But they might as well have been on Mars. Stevie and Meg had nice Mrs. Palmer, who often let her class out a few minutes early for recess, but Laura had Horrible Higgle, who sometimes took away the whole class's recess if some students didn't finish their work on time. Laura sure hoped they could learn their fractions in the twelve minutes before the bell rang.

She scrunched herself down behind Brent, and her thick brown hair fell in a curtain around her face. Now she felt hidden and private. She reached into her desk for the fat envelope she had put in there. It was Molly Quindlen's latest letter, which Laura had already read three times but just *had* to read again.

Laura unfolded the letter, careful not to make any crinkling sounds. She loved the idea that even though Molly, her friend, wasn't right there in class, Molly, her Friends 4-Ever pen pal, was.

Laura began reading:

Dear Laura (and Meg and Stevie, if you're reading this, too!!!),

I got three letters in one day, which was a good thing 'cause I was having a horrible day yesterday. It's still winter here. BORING! BORING! BORING! My dad said we won't even put out the rakes and grass seed for another couple of weeks at Grandpa's hardware store. People are still buying snow shovels!!!

I was looking at the memory book you guys gave me, and that reminded me of spring in Crispin Landing. I'll miss being in the dance recital at Miss Humphrey's and getting ready for the big tag sale. What dances are they doing in the recital, Laura? Do you have a big part? My favorite was when we were Snowflakes last year. I loved that costume the best. Too many rehearsals, but it was worth it!

4

So tell me all about the dance recital and about any super money-making schemes for the Crispin Landing Tag Sale (boo-hoo!). And tell me the latest fourth-grade news (including the bad stuff!!!). Even bad news from you guys is good news to me.

Speaking of bad news, the Terrible Three still can't stand that I'm friends with Kristy Pollard. I can't help it if my dad knew her dad practically since they were born. You know what Tammy, the Super Mean One, did? You won't believe it. She invited me to her birthday sleepover (probably her parents made her) but she put the wrong time down on the invitation, and I was two hours late! I hate them (not Kristy, who's still sooo nice), and if I ever have a party, I'm going to tell them the wrong year!

You guys are the Terrific Three, and I wish a tornado could blow Riggs and me all the way home to Crispin Landing. I'm counting the days!

Your Friend 4-Ever,

5

P.S. Thanks for the pink tulip petals from my old front yard. I put them with my 'N' Stuff. Lucy, our mail lady, said you guys have to put more stamps on the letters if there's 'N' Stuff inside, especially pebbles 'n' stuff like that. Got that, Meg? Lucy thinks our pen pal club is really neat. When I hear her little truck pull up to Grandpa's mailbox, I run right out and she tells me whether it's a cat day, a unicorn day, or a sneakers day. Yesterday, I got all three! Thanks guys.

Laura smiled. Sometimes Molly's P.S.'s were almost as long as the rest of the letter. She loved Molly's letters, but she loved the real Molly even more. Things just weren't the same since her friend had moved away nearly eight months before. It seemed like eight years since she had walked to school with Molly or taken ballet class with her. Laura thought of Molly every single day, sometimes more. Especially lately.

Lately things just weren't going a hundred percent right for Laura. No matter how hard she worked at school, some little thing seemed to go wrong. Like her science project dying on her before she could get the plants to school. Like not having any friends in ballet because Molly had always been her buddy in dance class. Like Meg suddenly deciding to play soccer with Stevie, when she knew Laura hated all that bumping and crashing into each other. Like her mother working full-time now and sending Laura to the After-School Program. That was the worst. She just hated being in school until five-thirty when practically everybody else had gone home. Even the principal!

Laura was so lost in her grumpy thoughts she didn't hear Mrs. Higgle rustling down the aisle until a shadow fell right over her desk.

"What is this, Laura?" Mrs. Higgle snatched Molly's letter from Laura's hand before she could slip it into her math book.

"It's . . . I . . . finished my math . . . so . . ." Laura began to explain.

"We have already covered letter-writing during Language Arts, Laura. This is math time. You will have to stay in for today's recess," Mrs. Higgle said. She walked away still clutching Molly's letter in her hand.

When the one-thirty recess bell rang, every chair but Laura's scraped against the linoleum floor. Kids rushed out of Mrs. Higgle's room as if it were on fire.

"Slow down! Slow down!" Mrs. Higgle yelled after them, but they were already out the door.

"You are to do an extra math page while I am out, Laura," Mrs. Higgle directed. "You should have been getting yourself ahead instead of reading *this*." She tossed Molly's precious letter across the desk. Laura quickly put it into her backpack before anything else happened to it. Mrs. Higgle left the room and shut the heavy door with a loud click.

The room was so quiet Laura could hear the soft tick of the clock strike the seconds. One second, two seconds, three seconds. Real recess always flew by, but a no-recess recess like this one seemed to last forever. Laura couldn't bring herself to pick up her pencil. She looked around the room. Everyone else's workbooks and pencils were scattered about just where kids had abandoned them. The green blackboard was covered with all the work the class had done that morning. The closed windows and doors didn't quite shut out the happy voices of students enjoying twenty minutes of fresh air and freedom

8

while Laura was stuck inside, breathing chalk dust.

Laura sighed. She wanted to sneak out Molly's letter one more time and write an answer back: "Help, I'm a fourth-grade prisoner!" She wanted to feel very sorry for herself, but she didn't bother. As her mother often pointed out, Mrs. Higgle picked on everyone. Today was her turn.

She flipped over her math page and began a row of problems. Then, right in the middle of trying to figure out how to divide two thirds by one third, she heard a knock on the classroom window, the pen pals knock. Tap. Tap, tap. Tap.

Stevie was making her Frankenstein face, that is, a lightly freckled Frankenstein face framed by a mop of long reddish blonde hair. Next to Stevie, Meg was mouthing: "Open the window! Open the window!" and waving her arms all over.

Laura's big brown eyes got huge and glowed with excitement. She looked around the room, then tiptoed over and cranked open the window.

"It's okay. Mrs. Higgle's patrolling the swings. You're safe," Meg whispered, her big blue eyes bright. "She can't see us."

That was for sure. Stevie and Meg had squeezed themselves between a row of tall evergreen bushes and the outside wall of the classroom. Meg had sprigs of evergreen poking out of her blonde curls every which way, and Stevie was shedding needles.

Stevie dug into her Red Sox jacket and pulled out a faded tennis ball. "If anyone comes, I'll say we were looking for this," she whispered, prepared for anything. "So what did you do, Laura? Tie up the teacher? Bring in firecrackers?"

"Sure, Stevie," Meg groaned. "I suppose that's why Laura got the Most Cooperative Third-Grader Award last year."

"And I got the Ants-In-Her-Pants Prize," Stevie laughed. "So why *did* you lose recess, Laura?"

"Mrs. Higgle caught me reading Molly's letter when I was supposed to be doing math."

"You should've told her it was part of a writing assignment," Stevie said, leaning her elbows on the windowsill. "You know, learning to write letters."

"Except she only lets us write fake letters," Laura grumbled. "Like ordering a washing machine or asking for free brochures from the state capital."

"What a waste," Stevie sighed. "I'm sure glad I didn't get her, or I would have missed a hundred recesses by now, the way Dave and Mike did. She hated my brothers."

"Did you at least get Molly's letter back?" Meg asked. "Bring it to our next Friends 4-Ever meeting."

"It's in my backpack. I was afraid she was going to read it out loud to the whole class like she usually does when kids have stuff they're not supposed to have. But she was in a rush to get out to the playground."

"Yeah, to make sure kids don't have too much fun," Stevie said.

"Hey, we'd better go before *we* lose recess," Meg interrupted. "See you later, Laura," Meg said as she and Stevie squeezed themselves back through the bushes.

When Laura heard the recess bell ring, she hurried back to her desk and rushed through half a page of math problems. She was hard at work when the kids drifted back in.

"Sorry about recess, Laura," Shana McCardle

11

whispered as she walked by Laura's desk. She dropped a small yellow piece of paper on Laura's desk before moving on.

Laura quickly unfolded Shana's note, which said: HANG IN THERE. Laura stuck the note in her pocket before she got caught again. Without turning around, she quickly gave Shana a thumbs up sign.

Shana was Laura's "sort of" friend. She and Laura rolled their eyes at each other when things got really bad in class. Sometimes they even sat at lunch together if Mrs. Higgle got the class to the cafeteria late. And Shana was the only student Laura knew in the After-School Program. She might have been even more than a "sort of" friend, but Meg and Stevie didn't seem to like her.

When the dismissal bell rang, Laura walked out of the class with Shana. "Thanks for the note. I hated missing recess. I should have known better," Laura sighed.

"It kinda makes me feel better that she picks on good kids, too," Shana said with a shake of her black spiky hair and her parrot earrings. "I mean, I probably *deserve* it since I don't remember to bring my homework half the time."

12

This was true. Even as Laura was jamming her three-ring binder and several different books into her backpack, Shana's skinny arms were completely empty. Laura never saw her carrying much more than a tiny spangled notebook or a couple of teen magazines. Maybe that's why she had to repeat fourth grade when she came to Crispin Landing Elementary. But Laura didn't care. She liked her "sort of" friend.

"Hey, Laura," Stevie said, landing with a crash right by Laura's locker with Meg trailing behind. "Hi, Shane."

"Oh, hi," Shana mumbled before moving off. "See you later, Laura."

"For the millionth time, Stevie, her name is Shana," Laura said, gritting her teeth, braces and all.

"What kind of a name is Shana?"

"Well, Stevie's kind of a weird name, too," Laura said, though deep down inside she knew Stevie's name was perfect for her. Much more perfect than her real name, Stephanie. Nobody ever called her *that*.

"It's not her name," Meg broke in. "It's her — "

"I know, it's her earrings," Laura answered.

"Why do we have to get into this dumb conversation about Shana all the time anyway?"

" 'Cause her earlobes are going to fall off if she wears any more junk on them," Stevie said, pulling on her own no-earring ears.

"And her hair's going to fall out from all that goop she uses to keep those spikes standing up," Meg answered. "I mean, if I had straight hair like hers — "

"Which you don't," Stevie interrupted, patting Meg's fuzzy blonde head.

"*If* I did," Meg continued, "I sure wouldn't cut the whole front half into those pointy spikes."

Laura sighed. "You two are lucky. You don't have to go to the After-School Program the way Shana and I do."

"You wouldn't have to, either, if you came to soccer," Meg pointed out.

"I don't like soccer!" Laura said. Of all people, Meg should have known that Laura couldn't do ballet *and* soccer *and* the piles of homework Mrs. Higgle gave every night.

"The soccer kids are great," Meg went on, caught up in her new sport.

"Yeah, not weird," Stevie added, pretending to kick a ball down the hall.

"Shana isn't weird. She's different, that's all," Laura said, defending her new friend.

"Yeah, different like an alien," Stevie said, and winked.

"Your brother Mike likes her well enough," Laura pointed out.

"He does not!" Stevie protested. "My brother hates girls, and even if he didn't, he wouldn't like one who wears tight black biker pants and earrings to school. She probably can't even ride a bike."

Meg laughed at the thought of Shana on a bike or doing any sport. Shana was the only fourth-grader who wore fake nails when it wasn't Halloween. "She probably thinks we're big babies or something. I can't figure out what you two have to talk about, Laura," Meg said. She shook her head, as puzzled as if Laura had adopted a Martian for a friend.

"She's nice to me, and she liked me in the *The Magic Princess*. We talk about dance and stuff," Laura said.

"I can't picture her in those little pink slippers," Stevie snorted. "She's more the MTV type."

"Maybe she is," Laura agreed, "but she knows lots of things from living all over."

"She doesn't know how to ride a bike, I bet," Stevie said. "And I know for sure she can't play outfield. She made our team lose in gym, remember?"

"Never mind her," Meg broke in. "Can I see Molly's letter now that you got it back from Horrible Higgle?"

"At the meeting, okay?" Laura answered.

Meg and Stevie looked at each other. The three girls always shared *everything*, even Molly's letters. At least most of the time.

"C'mon. What's the matter, Laura?" Meg wanted to know. "We usually tell each other everything, don't we?"

"Not everything," Laura said, surprising herself.

Before Meg could ask what Laura meant, Mrs. Whittaker came rushing down the hall, gathering up the After-School Program kids like stray chicks. "Time to go in, Lauren. Let's go," she said as she separated Laura from Stevie and Meg.

"It's Laura, not Lauren," Stevie chimed in.

"Yes, dear, now run along," Mrs. Whittaker told Meg and Stevie.

They turned and each gave Laura an I-feel-sorry-for-you look. Stevie pushed open the heavy lobby door, and she and Meg burst out into the bright spring sunshine. Laura watched them go, then turned toward the cafeteria, where the homework tables were all set up.

Molly didn't know the half of it, Laura thought. It might as well be winter here, too.

COOPED UP

Laura loved the bustling cafeteria at lunch when she and Meg and Stevie squeezed into the lunch line together so they could order identical lunches. They always sat at the same table in the same order, with Stevie on the end of the bench so she could stretch her legs out every other minute. The girls had a hard time not talking with food in their mouths, there was always so much to say.

But now, after school, the cafeteria was totally different. The smell of today's lunch, gluey orange macaroni and cheese, hung in the air. The colorful salad bar was gone, the big bowl of fresh fruit was gone, and the kitchen workers had pulled down the metal grill over the display cases. It was time for homework now, not time to go back for seconds or make a little volcano of mashed potatoes and gravy.

"Don't you just hate it?" Shana muttered. "They should call this the After-School Prison." She and Laura paused in the cafeteria doorway, their feet refusing to go any further.

"Let's get it over with," Laura groaned. She shifted her heavy purple backpack from one shoulder to the other. "Maybe we can sit together on the playground later."

"At least you don't have to be tooootored," Shana said, forming her lips into a little zero.

"Thank goodness," Laura agreed. Poor Shana had been to two schools before her parents were divorced, and she was still having trouble catching on to things at Crispin Landing Elementary. She didn't know what response cubes were in math, or that Albany was the capital of New York State. She found out about these things when Mrs. Higgle pointed them out, loudly, in

19

front of the whole class. Now Shana was getting tutored during part of the After-School Program so she could catch up.

"See you at four-fifteen," Shana said. She headed off to the corner of the cafeteria, where Mr. Juliano was waiting for her.

"Everyone take your seats for snack time," Mrs. Whittaker shouted. The little kids waited for the last possible minute to come to the homework tables, where exactly two slightly stale graham crackers and dark purple grape juice awaited each of them. How Laura wished it were Thursday, her mother's day off from the bookstore. Then she could hang out in her room or read a book on their big flowered couch if she wanted, and her snack would be something delicious her mother had made. Definitely not stale crackers! Why did her mother have to work so much, Laura wondered to herself.

"Yuck, these again!" Katie Nolon, a kindergartner, cried. "Double yuck!" agreed Charles Rowan, who looked like a Charlie but didn't want to be called that. Both children crumbled their crackers into dusty pieces the way they did every day.

Laura just wanted the so-called snack time to be over so she could get on with her homework, then talk with Shana. The worst thing about the After-School Program wasn't the stale crackers or the grape juice. It was being one of the oldest students there. The After-School Program was for *little kids*, and the whole school knew it.

"Rub and scrub, clean and sweep, into the barrel way down deep!" Mrs. Whittaker chirped to the kids at each table when snack time was over. Couldn't she see that not everyone was seven years old and could clean up without that silly song every day? Honestly!

Laura swallowed her warm purple juice in one gulp, then pitched her paper cup into the big green barrel. The juice was worse than cough medicine. She went back to the table and swept off the crumbs that the little kids always brushed onto the benches when they cleaned up.

"Kindergartners and first-graders, over here!" Mrs. Whittaker called from the reading corner, where colored rectangles of carpet were set up on the floor for the little kids.

The older After-Schoolers knew what they were supposed to do, but they did it as slowly

21

as possible. At each table, students got out their books, homework sheets, and pencils, and when they couldn't drag it out any longer, some of them actually got to work.

Laura didn't dawdle like the second- and third-graders. Homework was like the awful purple juice. It was best to get it out of the way fast! She opened her social studies book and tried to concentrate on the Constitutional Convention while Mrs. Whittaker asked the little kids: "And then what did the third billy goat do, boys and girls?"

As Laura read, a skinny line of sunshine began to spread across the table from the skylight over the cafeteria. She wanted to be out in that sunshine with Meg and Stevie, not trapped in a book with Ben Franklin. There was only one cure.

When she finished her chapter, Laura reached down into her backpack and pulled out her binder. Tucked in back was a small supply of her Friends 4-Ever stationery so she could write to Molly whenever she needed to talk to her friend. She smoothed out a sheet of the pale blue paper with its happy border of unicorns, and poured out her jumbled thoughts.

Dear Molly,

I know it's Stevie's turn to write, but she's out practicing soccer (again!!!) with Meg (again!!!). I'm in the cafeteria (again!!!) and trying not to hear Mrs. Whittaker reading fairy tales to the little kids.

I HATE BEING HERE!!! That's my Number One Problem. I did what you said and asked my mother if I could stay in our house alone on the days Meg and Stevie have practice. She says she doesn't want me to be a passkey or latchkey child, whatever that is. I wish she was still working part-time like last year, instead of RUINING MY LIFE!!! My mom doesn't care — even when I'm 29 I'll still have to be in the After-School Program! Reading your letters and writing to you is the only thing I can stand about it.

Well, not the only thing. There's my sec-

23

ond problem. *You know that girl I told you about, Shana? The one who calls this The After-School Prison? She's stuck here, too, but not because her mother treats her like a baby. Just the opposite. She's allowed to go to town by herself. Anyway, Shana gets tutored so she can ketchup (Ha! Ha! Just kidding! I mean catch up!!!). Shana's ten already, and she's the only other person here who's older than I am. Anyway, we get to talk in the playground when they let us out for air. (Today it smells like macaroni and cheese in here, just as rubbery as last year, in case you're wondering, with that yucky brown crust on top. I think I'm going to be sick!!!!)*

Back to Shana. Meg and Stevie make fun of her because they don't like her hair (which is half spiky on top but long in back). I thought it was weird at first, too, but now I'm used to it and who cares anyway???? But she's not weird, that's the main thing. They're kind of mean to her and don't even say her name right and they just think I'm stuck with her like I'm stuck in the After-School Program. But I like her the rest of the time, too, and wish she could sit with us at lunch. But Meg and Stevie always spread out and pretend she's invisible when we walk to the table with our trays, so she goes some- place else.

How can I get them to be nice to her? All they do is blab about soccer and they never LISTEN!!!! Help!

Your Friend 4-Ever,

Laura

P.S. Here's a nature sticker I got in science today. At least Mr. Juliano thinks I'm smart, not like you-know-who.
P.P.S. I can't believe The Terrible Three are still bugging you. Maybe a tornado will blow them away from Kansas!

There. Now Laura felt much better. She folded her letter neatly into three even sections and tucked in the blue jay sticker she had gotten for the second-highest mark on the bird paper in Science.

"Is that a love letter?" Shana asked when she

walked up just as Laura was licking the envelope.

"Um. Well. Um." Laura giggled in embarrassment. In fact, she did love Molly, but this wasn't the kind of love letter Shana was teasing about. "No, just a regular letter."

The girls sat, half hanging off the bench, and waited for Mrs. Whittaker to announce the next activity. "Playground time! Playground, boys and girls. Get your coats from your cubbies and line up!"

"Can't she say lockers instead of cubbies? Fourth-graders don't have cubbies anymore," Laura muttered, thinking about her shiny red locker with the little mirror inside and the photo magnets of Meg and Stevie and Molly. Lockers were the only good thing about fourth grade, and Laura didn't want anyone to think she still had an open cubby like last year. "I just hope we don't see anyone from our class."

Laura and Shana dragged themselves to the back of the playground line.

"Please, children, find your buddy. K's, then first-graders, then the older grades. Please! A straight line, please!" Mrs. Whittaker repeated as the younger children squirmed into their jackets.

The sun warmed the girls as they walked out. They lifted their faces and closed their eyes for a second, feeling like cats taking a good long stretch after being indoors.

"Oh, no! Don't look now," Laura groaned when she opened her eyes. "There's Mike Ames and some other sixth-graders. They *would* have to show up now!"

"Ride 'em Ryder," Stevie's brother Mike called out to Laura as he zoomed by on his bike with several other boys. "Got your buddy with you?" he asked for all his own buddies to hear.

Laura felt her cheeks go hot and red right along with her ears. She bent her head forward so that she could hide inside her hair.

"Come a little closer, and you'll get paired off buddy-buddy, too!" Shana yelled back boldly.

The boys all laughed, and Mike turned around to see if Shana noticed him doing wheelies and skids around the edge of the parking lot. No matter what Stevie said, Laura could see Mike kind of liked Shana. Even if she wasn't so hot in sports.

"Show-offs!" Shana sniffed. "Mike Ames thinks he's so cool, but he's not."

Laura didn't know what to say about Stevie's brother. If she hadn't been walking with Shana, Mike would have biked by without even noticing Laura. He never showed off for *her*.

"He's all right," Laura mumbled loyally.

"Guess you have to like him," Shana began, "I mean, since he's Stevie's brother and all."

"Um, I don't think about it," Laura said. "He's just there."

This was true. Laura didn't think about boys much except when they hogged the little circle at the end of Half Moon Lane, where Stevie lived. They barely moved if the girls wanted to use the circle to skate or ride their own bikes. Half the time they didn't even notice cars coming down the road. Shana was the first girl Laura knew whom the boys seemed to notice. Maybe it was her earrings.

Laura and Shana went to their spot in the playground, a set of steps that led down to the lower parking lot where the teachers parked their cars. Sometimes Laura wanted to dangle from the swings or the climbing bars in the play-ground the way the girls often did in Meg's backyard, but here at school it seemed too babyish.

"I forgot to bring my new *Top Teens*. It has the coolest picture of Kirk Kennedy. You know. He's in *All Grown Up*."

"I know," Laura said, as if Kirk Kennedy was practically her best friend.

Shana kept a stack of teen magazines in her locker and loved to look at the pictures again and again. The only magazine Laura got was *Ranger Rick*, which she still liked if they had a koala or penguin on the cover, but she could hardly drool over those!

"We can just hang out 'til they set us free," Laura joked.

Shana sat on the bottom step and formed her initials in the gravel with the toe of one of her studded black flats. "Did Mrs. Higgle ever give you back that letter she took from you during math today?"

"Yeah, I guess I got lucky. She could have read it out loud like she did with Rachel's note last week. I would have died!" Laura said. She got a little red just thinking about it.

"Why? Who was it from?"

"Molly Quindlen, you know, my friend who moved to Kansas?" Laura said quietly. She hoped Shana wouldn't keep asking about the letter. Suddenly the Friends 4-Ever club seemed kind of babyish — like getting *Ranger Rick*.

"Is that who you were writing to during study time today?"

"Yeah, even though it wasn't my turn to write," Laura blurted out. "I mean, I can write her anytime, but usually I write on Wednesdays but — "

Shana stopped doodling with her foot and looked up at Laura, puzzled. "You have to write on a certain day? Is it part of some secret club or chain letter or something?"

"Sort of," Laura said. "See, Molly, Meg, and Stevie, and I used to do everything together, before last year, I mean. Then Molly had to go to her grandfather's in Kansas 'cause he's sick. We were kind of upset, I mean *real* upset, so we promised to write to her once a week. We started kind of a pen pals club with special stationery so she'd have lots of letters and . . ."

Laura stopped talking. What if Shana laughed and thought it was dumb to have special paper and rules about writing?

"Is that why you have matching paper and all?" Shana asked.

30

"Sort of. I mean it doesn't match exactly. Mine's got unicorns, Molly has rainbows, Meg has kittens, and Stevie has — "

"A basketball hoop?" Shana said.

"Almost. High-top sneakers."

Shana dangled her shoe off the end of her foot and tried to twirl it around. "Molly's lucky."

"Why?" Laura was shocked. "She cried every night before she left and for a long time after she got out there."

"I mean lucky 'cause you guys stayed her friends and still write to her and all. I haven't even gotten a postcard from the kids I knew in Florida or in Texas, where we were before. Every time we move I have to start all over. And not just in math."

"That must be so awful," Laura said.

"Everybody's always got their own groups already, know what I mean?" Shana went on, almost as if she were talking to herself.

Now Laura couldn't say a word. The Friends 4-Ever had always been just Molly, Stevie, Meg, and Laura. Even before they had a name or a club.

"I can tell Meg and Stevie don't like me," Shana said next.

"Sure they do," Laura said feebly. But inside she knew the truth: Meg and Stevie *didn't* like Shana much. Worse, they didn't even think about her.

"No they don't. You're the only one who's nice to me, and that's because we're stuck in Horrible Higgle's and here," Shana answered as she poked at the ground with her foot.

"Lauren! Lauren Ryder? Your mother is here," Laura heard next.

Sure enough, the Ryders' blue Chevy had just pulled into the school parking lot.

"I've gotta go. My mom is here," Laura said. "See you tomorrow."

"Sure."

Laura couldn't wait to get away. She didn't like being reminded that the only time she hung out with Shana was when her two *real* friends, Meg and Stevie, weren't around. She didn't like this awful new feeling of being what her mother would call a "Fair Weather Friend." Laura knew if you weren't a friend all the time, you weren't someone's real friend at all.

MIXED-UP MEETING

Warburton Avenue was one big traffic jam when school got out at 3:15. Big yellow buses and small yellow vans wound their way around Crispin Landing Elementary School as frantic teachers tried to keep the right kids from getting on the wrong bus. Inside, students jammed the hallways as they looked for stray backpacks, slammed their lockers for the last time that day, and searched a sea of heads for their friends.

Finally it was Thursday, Laura's favorite day of the week. The minute the bell rang, she was free. No After-School Prison on Thursday. Just a quick walk home with Meg and Stevie, then a meeting of Friends 4-Ever to catch up on Molly's letters and have fun. For a change, the girls were going to meet at Laura's house, and she couldn't wait.

"Hey, Mrs. Higgle actually let you out on time," Stevie said when Laura reached her locker.

"I know. I know," Laura said. "More time for us. Did you get your work done, Stevie?"

"I made her do it during recess," Meg piped up before Stevie could answer. "Watch this. How do you spell 'occasion,' Stevie?"

Stevie was busy trying to jam her locker shut, which wasn't easy since a shoelace and what looked like part of a banana peel were sticking out. Then she rolled her eyes upward as if the spelling word were written on the ceiling. "O - C - A- . . . no, I mean, O - C - C - A - . . . um, um . . . "

"Stevie!" Meg cried. "Think, think!"

"O - C - C - A - S - I - O - N! Now can I go home, Teach?"

"Whew! Honestly, Stevie, just remember that for the test tomorrow, okay?"

"You guys are sooo lucky," Laura said. "You

know what's on my list? 'Liverwurst'! Mrs. Higgle thinks the regular spelling list is too easy."

"Well, I hope you only have to spell it, not eat it," Stevie laughed.

"L - I - V - E - R - W - U - R - S - T. Blech!" Laura said, stretching out her tongue.

"Let's go," Meg said. She grabbed her jacket and tried to stuff it into her backpack without any success. Instead she tied the jacket arms around her waist, and Laura and Stevie did the same with theirs.

The girls walked in step down the hall, passed the cafeteria, and pushed together on the silver bar of the lobby door. Just then Laura caught a glimpse of Shana and gave her a tiny wave. But Shana just kept walking on without waving back.

"Aren't you glad today's Thursday and you can just go straight home?" Meg asked.

"Sort of," Laura answered, feeling a little pang inside. "Shana's not going to have anybody to talk with."

"Well, she must have had somebody before you started going," Meg said, as if that settled the problem.

"No, she didn't. See, all the other After-

Schoolers are . . . " Laura began, but Meg was rushing after Stevie and not listening anymore. Laura turned back and saw Shana shuffle into the cafeteria, alone. Though kids had to stream around Laura to get by, she stood in the middle of the hallway, confused for a second about where to go. Finally, she headed outside and looked for Stevie and Meg. They were already halfway across the lawn in front of the school when Laura caught up with them.

"I hope Joe Pat isn't the crossing guard today," Stevie was saying.

"No such luck," Meg groaned. She pointed to the white-haired man who was already stopping traffic in every direction to get kids across Warburton Avenue. Joe Pat liked nothing better than to create a long line of traffic at the corner of Warburton and Crispin Landing Road. The madder the drivers got, the longer Joe Pat held up his big yellow stop sign.

"He's doing make-way-for-ducklings again," Stevie muttered. "I mean, how come a half hour after school lets out I can ride my bike or skateboard all over the place, but when I leave school he has to march us across the road?"

Crossing the busy intersection, all three girls

kept their eyes to the ground. Maybe if they didn't look at the cars, the drivers wouldn't notice the three fourth-graders standing a head taller than most of the other children going across.

When they reached the other side, Stevie swung herself around the lamp post a few times and hurled herself into Crispin Landing Road. This was something she did every day, as if she were unwinding herself from school.

And the way she did every day, Meg looked for Patches, a calico cat who often greeted the girls when they came home. "There she is," Meg and Laura cried together when Patches popped out from some bushes and presented her fuzzy belly to the girls. For a minute this helped Laura leave school behind and get herself in the mood for an afternoon with her best and oldest friends.

"There, there," Laura crooned as the cat lay on her back and lifted her chin for a good tickle.

"C'mon, let's go say hi to Molly's house," Stevie said when the cat rubbing ended.

The girls quickly ran down Half Moon Lane to Molly's old house and yelled out "Hi, Molly!" This was something they still did almost every day since Molly had moved away. If they were lucky, Mrs. Hansen, the lovely old woman who lived there now, would wave back and sometimes even offer the girls something to eat. But today the three girls just waved and whizzed by, then turned back toward Crispin Landing Road, where Laura's house was.

"Molly wrote to all three of us," Laura announced when they got to the corner. "She said she got three of our letters in one day."

"Are the Terrible Three still on the warpath?" Stevie asked. "In my last letter, I told her she should stuff their lockers with hay."

"I can't believe they are so mean to Molly," Meg said. "You'd think by now they'd know how great she is. They must be sooo dumb."

All three girls inhaled and exhaled an angry breath at the same time just thinking about it.

"I guess we'd better get back on our writing schedule," Meg, the organizer, said. "Molly shouldn't be getting three letters in one day."

"What difference does it make, Meg?" Stevie asked. She rolled her eyes as if Meg had just assigned her three book reports.

"What if you were Molly and you were waiting on a certain day for a certain letter from a certain friend?" Meg asked.

38

"I'd certainly get kind of cold and wet waiting by the mailbox," Stevie answered.

When the girls rounded the blind curve near Laura's house, all three girls hopped on the curb. Ever since they could walk, their parents had lectured them about how drivers couldn't see pedestrians around that curve.

"Blah, blah, blah. Blah, blah, blah," the girls singsonged together, imitating all the warnings as they balanced themselves on the curb.

Laura hoped her mother was watching. Maybe if she could see how careful Laura was about the road, she would give in and let Laura come home after school instead of going to the After-School Program.

No such luck. Mrs. Ryder was busy in the kitchen when the girls walked in. "No mail," she called out as Laura flipped through the magazines and bills lying on the coffee table. Maybe a Molly letter was mixed in with the Giant Foods flyer.

"Anything?" Meg asked from over Laura's shoulder.

Laura shook her head. "Nope."

"Well, at least your mom made cookies," Stevie said, sniffing the air.

Sure enough, a warm buttery smell greeted the girls when they went into the kitchen. The girls didn't often meet at Laura's now that Mrs. Ryder worked full-time. Also their little rented house was small for Laura's friends, who tended to spread all over the place with big backpacks, jackets, and all the things they liked to bring to their meetings.

"What are you up to today, girls?" Mrs. Ryder asked when the girls squeezed themselves into chairs in the tiny kitchen.

"Writing letters, of course," Meg began. "Then we have to plan our booth for the tag sale."

"Well, I hope you girls sell more than you buy," Mrs. Ryder said. "Last year Laura put all her profits into more toys."

"I did not!" Laura protested, even though this was true. She, Meg, Molly, and Stevie had sold the few things they could part with but then turned around and went from yard to yard buying old buttons, games with missing pieces, junk jewelry, and even a pair of dusty ceramic pilgrims, which none of the mothers wanted to display on Thanksgiving.

"This year we really, really are going to get

rid of everything," Stevie began, "and use the money to get — "

Meg sputtered and nearly tipped over her glass of milk. She reached her leg under the table to stop Stevie from saying anything else.

" — some stuff . . . " Stevie trailed off.

The girls had been cooking up a scheme ever since they helped Molly pack up the summer before. To make Molly feel a little better about moving, her parents let her sell some of her toys and use the money to get a phone. Ever since, the other three Friends 4-Ever could think of nothing else. Not that their parents knew anything about this latest idea, of course. Laura was pretty sure her mother would probably feel the same way about a phone as she did about pierced ears, MTV, and makeup kits — too old and too expensive. Good thing Stevie hadn't blabbed it out.

"Well, I certainly won't talk you girls out of selling some of your things. We could use the space," Mrs. Ryder sighed. "I don't know how Laura can even turn around in her room."

"I like my room just the way it is!" Laura cried. Every inch, she thought to herself as she formed her lovely dark eyebrows into a frown. She was

41

getting worried that her mother's full-time job was the first step to buying a bigger house in a different neighborhood. Laura didn't want any more changes. It was bad enough that Molly was gone.

Mrs. Ryder's own brown eyebrows shot up in surprise at this announcement since Laura was always complaining about how small her room was. "You girls can have your meeting in the attic if you need more space. It's still a bit chilly up there, but it might be more fun."

"We're going to meet in my room," Laura said firmly.

Meg and Stevie looked at each other. When they did go to Laura's, they preferred meeting in the unfinished attic space, where they could fix it up with empty boxes and dividers made out of old blankets. Then they liked to pretend they were living together in their own apartment, away from parents who thought they were too young to get telephones.

Laura's room was a bit of a squeeze what with the girls' long legs and bony elbows. But it was cozy, too. Laura's Aunt Ev had painted fluffy clouds on the pale blue walls when they moved in. Like Molly, Laura had ballet posters on the wall, and the dancers seemed to glide across the sky. Aunt Ev had even bought Laura a pair of white satin toe shoes autographed by the Sugar Plum Fairy in a performance of *The Nutcracker* the Christmas before. The ballet shoes hung right over Laura's white bed along with framed pictures of Laura at different dance recitals.

"I've got the bed," Stevie said, hurling herself across it. Laura and Meg each found a spot on the floor and took out their clipboards.

"We've got a lot of things to do," Meg said. "We have to make some lists."

Stevie threw a stuffed monkey at Meg's head. "Then we have to make lists of the lists," Stevie said, imitating Meg's voice. "Then lists of those — "

"We heard you, we heard you," Meg scolded. "It's time for the meeting. I hereby call to order the meeting of the Friends 4-Ever pen pals. Laura Ryder will read Molly's latest letter."

Laura unfolded the letter and read it slowly and carefully. She knew the words practically by heart and knew just where to pause and where to speak louder so Stevie and Meg could enjoy it, too. This was part of the meetings she loved. Sharing Molly's words out loud was the next best thing to having Molly right there.

"I wish the Terrible Three would come here," Stevie said when Laura finished Molly's letter. "I'd get my brothers and their friends to make them miserable. Then they'd find out what it's like to be left out!"

Meg nodded in complete agreement. "Poor Molly. No wonder she can't wait to get home."

"To us," Stevie said with a big grin.

"So what *are* you going to be in the ballet recital, Laura?" Meg wanted to know when they finished discussing the Terrible Three.

"I'm not going to be anything," Laura mumbled.

Stevie bounced up from where she was sitting. "It ought to be easy making a costume for that!"

"But . . . but you've been in the recital every year," Meg sputtered. "You can't miss it this year!"

"I know, but I don't care," Laura said, jutting her chin out. This was not the Laura her friends were used to. "Ballet's no fun without Molly. I might not take it after this session. I've got too much homework, and I never have any time now that I have to go to the After-School Program, too. I hate getting up and going to ballet class on Saturday mornings. I just hate it!"

Meg and Stevie stared at each other with wide eyes. They didn't know the first thing about *pliés* or all those other French words for moving your feet or waving your arms around. But ballet was as much a part of Laura as her brown eyes and graceful way of walking.

"What about all your ballet stuff, Laura?" Stevie asked.

"I'm selling it all at the tag sale," Laura blurted out. She didn't dare look at the small fur *Nutcracker* mouse she'd gotten in her stocking a couple of Christmases ago, or at the purple dance bag her parents had given her on her last birthday to carry her clothes to ballet class. No, she just looked straight ahead and tried not to think about any of it.

"Laura, you are not yourself," Meg said, as if her best friend had just broken out into chicken pox right there, and Meg was the doctor.

"Then who is she?" Stevie cried. "Wonder Woman? Lassie? Who?"

Laura didn't laugh. She didn't even smile. She *wasn't* herself lately. She was tired of always being Most Cooperative Laura, who just went along with everyone else's plans. She was tired of people telling her she should go to soccer, go to ballet, go to the After-School Program.

"Never mind," Laura said. "Let's just write our letters, okay?" She leaned back against the wall, mad at herself for spoiling the meeting.

"Okay, sure, if that's what you want," Meg said quietly. "'I guess we ought to get back to the meeting, I mean, letter writing." Then she added, "I owe Molly a letter anyway."

In a few minutes the room was filled with the usual letter-writing sounds of breathing, erasing, scratching words out, and scribbling in others.

After filling up two sheets and sneaking a look at Stevie's letter, Meg felt a little better. Maybe the meeting was going to be okay after all. At least that's what she hoped. Then she noticed Laura was still staring straight ahead, her clipboard untouched on the floor.

"Laura, how come you're not writing?" Meg asked.

"I, um . . . just remembered . . . I already wrote Molly a letter, the other day. During the After-School Program."

"Well, where is it?" Meg wanted to know.

"I . . . uh . . . mailed it already," Laura said.

"I thought we weren't going to have any more

secret letters," Meg continued, "since we're all friends with Molly. Remember what happened last fall when Stevie sent Molly a secret letter?"

Stevie groaned from where she was lying on the floor. "Meg! We didn't swear in blood we wouldn't write to Molly without blabbing it all over the neighbhorhood."

"I know, Stevie, but if you'd told me and Laura about how left out you felt when we auditioned for *The Magic Princess*, we could've made you feel better right away instead of waiting for Molly to tell you what to do," Meg pointed out. "I thought we were going to share all our letters so we would stay friends just the way we were before Molly moved. No secrets or anything, you know?"

The room was quiet. Stevie even stopped snapping her gum.

"If we're a club, then we have to do things the way we said," Meg continued. She sat up straight and made herself taller than she already was. "We have to have rules, and jobs, and share," she said in a quivery voice.

Now Laura just wanted the meeting to be over. This arguing kept happening now that there were just three, not four, Friends 4-Ever right there. Before Molly went to Kansas, Laura and Meg stuck together and so did Stevie and Molly. Now there was always a leftover, and lately Laura was it.

"Well, maybe we don't have to stick to the rules exactly," Meg said hopefully. "Can you at least tell us what your letter said, Laura?"

"Unless you said something terrible about us, Laura," Stevie laughed.

"Nope, I just told her about Shana, that's all," Laura said truthfully.

"Shana?" Meg cried. "That girl in your class?"

Now Laura could feel her face getting hot with anger. This just proved that Stevie and Meg didn't even try to think about what it was like to be in Horrible Higgle's class and go to the After-School Program and not be able to play soccer. Didn't they ever think about Laura when she wasn't with them?

"Never mind," Laura said quietly, her anger turning to plain sadness.

"Hey, Laura, I could teach you soccer," Stevie said. "It's so easy. Then you wouldn't have to stay after school and hang out with what-sername."

"For the millionth time, I don't even want to

be in soccer, so would you two just quit talking about it? That's not the problem," Laura said, her voice cracking.

"Then what is, Laura?" Meg asked. "We're still your friends, and so's Molly. The year's almost over, and soccer's only a few more weeks, and we'll do the tag sale together. You won't need to be with Shana so much."

"I *like* being with her," Laura said stubbornly. "She's nice, and if you two would give her a chance, you'd find out what she's like."

"I already know what she's like, chasing my brother and wearing those stupid shoes, and pants, and all kinds of weird stuff."

"She does not chase Mike, Stevie!" Laura said. "The other day he rode his bike by us in the parking lot and was showing off in front of her."

"No way!" Stevie cried. She flipped onto her back and did bicycling motions in the air.

"It's true," Laura said.

"It doesn't matter if it's true or not, you two!" Meg interrupted. "I don't even know why we're even talking about somebody Laura's stuck with when we're supposed to be writing to Molly and planning the tag sale. Remember that, guys?"

"Can I stop this meeting for a second?" Laura

asked. "I'm not stuck with Shana. That's number one. You just don't know her yet and — "

"And we don't want to," Stevie said with a low giggle.

"Let me talk, it's my turn," Laura continued. "In a way, Shana is like Molly was when she got out to Kansas."

"Shana? Like Molly?" Stevie cried. "C'mon Laura. Get real."

Laura swallowed hard. She was usually the quiet, sweet one in the group and wasn't used to talking back to Meg and Stevie. "I told Shana about our club the other day, about how we thought it up so we could still be friends with Molly," Laura began. "She says she doesn't even get a postcard from the kids she left in Florida and in Texas, where she lived before that."

"She probably chased all their brothers," Stevie muttered.

"Stevie! I'm not finished," Laura said firmly. "Anyway, why can't we get other pen pals in Friends 4-Ever, not just us?" Laura asked.

" 'Cause then it wouldn't be four friends, get it?" Stevie said, feeling very pleased with herself. "I mean Friends 5-Ever or Friends 12-Ever? That sounds pretty dumb to me."

50

"Stevie's right," Meg said. "It was just supposed to be the four of us, so we could stay the same way we always were."

"But we're not the same as we were!" Laura cried. "Molly and I used to go to ballet together, now I have to go by myself. You never played soccer, and now you're never home. I never had to go to the After-School Program and now I do. I just wish . . ." Laura paused. What did she wish anyway? "I just wish Shana could come to one of our meetings, and we could help her write to some of *her* old friends."

Meg and Stevie looked at each other as if Laura had suggested inviting an armadillo to join their group. What was going on with Laura anyway? They could see Laura was near tears over this girl they didn't even know or want to know. This wasn't the same old Laura who went along with everything.

Now Laura seemed to have some plans of her own.

RAINY SATURDAY

Laura stared out at the kitchen window and watched the steady rain streak down the panes without any letup. She had a long Saturday ahead. They're avoiding me, she thought to herself as she pushed her hot cereal around in her bowl. Stevie, who hated shopping more than she hated writing letters, was going to the new mall in Roxbury. And Meg *said* she was going to Providence with her parents and her cousin. They're probably both at Meg's, Laura told herself. Without me. Having fun.

"Hey, Laura Elizabeth, something wrong with

my cooking? You look awfully mad at that cereal," Mr. Ryder said, interrupting Laura's conversation with herself.

"It's good, Dad, but . . ."

"But you're not a morning peanut, are you?" her father said gently.

Laura nodded. Might as well let her dad think she wasn't hungry in the morning. How could she explain that she'd ruined the Friends 4-Ever meeting two days ago, and now her friends had gone off to do things without her?

"Is it almost time for Pee Wee?" Laura asked, changing the subject.

"It's not time for cereal, I can see that. You go and turn on the television. I'm just going to heat up more coffee, and I'll be right in."

"It's a repeat," Laura called out to her father when the show came on. "The one about pen pals."

Laura knew just what her father would say next in his Pee Wee voice: "If you want to get a letter, you have to write a letter."

Laura had seen the Pee Wee Herman pen pal episode before. In fact, Meg even had a tape of it at her house, and the Friends 4-Ever knew all the lines by heart. But today it didn't seem as funny as usual. This morning, Mr. Ryder was the only one saying the lines out loud.

"Time to get ready for ballet," Mr. Ryder said when the credits came on at the end.

Laura let out the loudest sigh she could get away with when she heard that. "Do I have to go?"

"At ten dollars an hour you have to go," her father answered, just the way he had the last few Saturdays. "How come you're not leaping around the way you used to on Saturdays anyway?"

"I wish Molly were here," Laura grumbled.

"So do I. Then Bill Quindlen could drive on Saturdays," Mr. Ryder said as Laura made her way to her room as slowly as possible. "Mom's working extra hard so you can have these lessons, you know."

"I know," Laura said. But she wished she didn't know anything of the kind. Everything was the opposite of the way it used to be. Her nylon leotard and tights felt scratchy and twisty. She couldn't get her long hair into a nice smooth bun the way her mother always did.

When Laura glimpsed herself in the mirror, she hardly looked like the ballerina in the

"Snowflakes" dance at last year's recital. And, of course, her favorite other dancing Snowflake was two thousand miles away in Kansas.

Laura looked at a picture on her dresser. There were she and Molly together, all made up for the show and glittering in their white-and-silver-sequined tutus. "When are you coming home?" Laura whispered.

"I'll warm up the car," Mr. Ryder called before heading out the door.

Laura barely had time to pull her pink dancing slippers from a heap of shoes by the bed, let alone run a comb through her hair, stuff her clothes into her dance bag, and meet her dad out front.

Minutes later, she and her dad were doing something they also did every Saturday, circling the block to find a parking place. "I'd better let you out here," Mr. Ryder said finally. "If I'm not inside when class gets out, just look for me from the front door, okay?"

"Oh, fine," Laura muttered.

"Laura, come on now, do a few jets into the building," Mr. Ryder urged.

"They're *jetés*, Dad, not jets," Laura said. She pulled open the car door and dashed down the tiny alley toward the door that said "Miss Humphrey's Dance Studio." She could already hear Miss Humphrey repeating: "First position, hold, now second. That's it. Now hold again."

Laura dumped her bag and jacket in the changing room, raced down the hall, then tried to slip into the studio without anyone noticing. Of course, the mirrored wall doubled Laura's late arrival.

Laura tiptoed to the back line and slipped in between Katherine Hawes and Renee Clery, two older girls who always remembered to put up their hair in perfectly smooth buns. Laura lined herself up behind the dancer in front of her and hoped she could copy her movements until she caught the rhythm herself.

"Let's start again," Miss Humphrey said. She scratched the needle back to the beginning of the record.

With each exercise, Laura was just a second off. To unscramble her brain, she tried to picture Diana's Pool, a small pond she and Meg's family sometimes hiked to. No luck. Her leg came down when it was supposed to go up. She imagined a small fawn drinking from the pond, but still her movements didn't match what Miss Humphrey and the music were saying.

Ballet II was so much harder than Ballet Prep and Ballet I, which Laura had taken with Molly for several years. Molly and Laura had bravely signed up for the harder class, but now Laura felt lonely among so many older girls.

As the class went on, Laura got worse, not better. Besides that, she got that shrimpy feeling she hated, knowing she was the shortest girl in the group. She needed Molly there to make her feel old enough to be in Ballet II. But Molly was probably out horseback riding or something, Laura thought as she rushed through the last *port de bras.*

"We're going to stop a bit early today," Miss Humphrey announced. "I want to discuss the June recital. It will be here before you know it."

"Here are the practice schedules, girls," Miss Humphrey said when she turned off the record player. "Pass them around, then look them over. You'll see that we have two practice periods a day to choose from. You only need to come for two practices a week during May, then every day for the two weeks before the recital. This year we tried very hard to be more flexible."

Now "flexible" was just what Laura didn't want to be. Her heart sank when she noticed all the "flexible" practice times at six o'clock.

"Several of your parents who work made the very sensible suggestion about having later rehearsal times this year so you can still be in the show," Miss Humphrey said as she straightened her back even more than usual.

Laura knew that her own mother was one of those sensible parents Miss Humphrey was talking about. Laura felt herself deflate and her spine collapse at the thought of more hard dance classes, rehearsals, and another show, all of it without Molly.

"Miss Humphrey? Miss Humphrey?" Renee Clery called out.

"Yes, Renee."

"What is our group going to dance this year?" Renee asked.

Miss Humphrey smiled. "Our theme this year is 'Nocturne.' "

"Ooo," several of the girls said, pleased that this year they no longer had to *be* something like a snowflake or a Raggedy Ann. Nocturne? Nocturne? Laura kept asking herself. What on earth was that?

"See you next week, girls. Now don't forget to go over this with your parents and be ready to sign up for practice next Saturday," Miss Humphrey said as a new group of girls pressed into the doorway for the next class.

Laura walked out of the studio alone and crumpled the dreaded schedule into her dance bag as soon as she got to the changing room.

"I'm glad we don't have to be those silly Snowflakes again," one of the older girls said as she peeled down her leg warmers.

"Me, too," another girl answered, gliding dreamily to the window. "This will be sooo romantic."

"I hope we're partners," Katherine Hawes said to Renee.

"Let's ask my mom if we can go to Bella's today, okay?" someone else said.

Laura remembered when she and Molly chattered away like that as they got into street clothes after a hard workout at ballet. Often the two of them would come out of the ballet school, all warm, flushed, and excited, then go off for lunch at Bella's like some of the girls were about to do now.

Laura slumped inside the door frame of the small building and waited for her father to come by. The rain dripped in front of her as the other girls ran together to warm, dry cars, full of plans for the rainy afternoon. She was so lost in her own thoughts that she didn't hear the horn of her dad's car until he leaned on it for the third time.

"The parking around here gets worse every week," Mr. Ryder said when Laura got in the car. "Sorry you had to wait. I thought I had a spot, but one of the other ballet chauffeurs beat me to it. Parking's another thing I'm not so hot at. Like the cereal."

"It's okay, Dad. I liked your Pee Wee imitation," Laura said. She tried to make her father feel better about cooking breakfast and finding good parking places so she didn't have to think about ballet anymore.

"Hey, look what came while you were out," Mr. Ryder said. He pointed to the floor of the car.

"A wet newspaper?" Laura asked, puzzled.

"No, peanut, under that. A letter from your number one pen pal."

Laura bent down, seat belt and all, and searched through the pile of damp mail her father had thrown into the car. Sure enough, there was a rainbow-trimmed blue envelope with Laura's name in huge letters on the front.

"Oh, great, a letter from Molly!" Laura cried. She held the envelope in her hands like a present.

"I have to run into Ross's Hardware and get some trim paint for the front door. There's a space right out front, so you can stay out here and read your letter. Unless you want to shop for wrenches and wing nuts."

Laura was so busy tearing open Molly's envelope that she didn't answer or even hear the door slam. Instead, she sat in the car and unfolded Molly's latest letter as the rain beat down on the roof and her breath fogged up the windows:

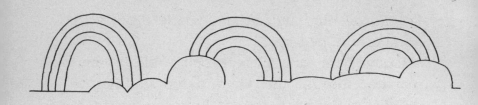

Dear Laura,

I love getting your letters, even the ones with problems! I'm glad you have Shana for a friend. With Mrs. Higgle you need one! Shana sounds really neat. I wish I could meet her. We'd have a lot to talk about, like how hard it is to fit in a new place.

Meg and Stevie are just being Meg and Stevie. You know how Meg is. She thinks that the latest thing she's doing is the most fun, and everybody else should be doing the same thing, too. I bet she's got the whole soccer team organized! Stevie doesn't sit still long enough to notice things. That's probably why she doesn't know you're miserable about school this year.

Maybe you should just bring Shana to the next meeting and see what happens. You could all help Shana write to one of her old friends. Maybe if Meg and Stevie got to know her, they would like her. She probably knows lots of neat things from living in different places (like alligator wrestling) that Meg and Stevie might like.

We had a picnic in the snow like we used to do at Meg's, and some of the kids thought it was a super idea — not the Terrible Three, though!!! They were too busy to come.

I'm still working on getting them to like me. If Kristy is with them, they just talk to her and pretend I'm not there. Kristy's so sweet and quiet (just like you) that she can't really tell them off. They wouldn't listen anyway.

You still didn't tell me about ballet. I miss it so much since they don't have classes near here. I hope I don't forget the movements!

You didn't mention the tag sale, either, but Meg and Stevie told me about it. (Is something else besides the Shana problem bugging you, Laura? Tell me next time, okay?)

Your Friend 4-Ever,

Molly

Laura reread the letter twice. Maybe Molly was right. Maybe she should just barge in with Shana. Once Meg and Stevie saw how nice she was, maybe they would be nicer, too.

"Hey, that must have been some letter," her father said when he slid into the front seat and Laura didn't even look up.

"Hmm," Laura answered. She was thinking hard about what to do.

The windshield wipers swept back and forth almost hypnotizing her. When they went one way, she decided she would bring Shana to the next meeting. When they went the other way, she decided it was a terrible idea.

A SURPRISE INVITATION

All of Crispin Landing Elementary School seemed soggy after five straight days of rain. The children's plastic slickers, the little kids' boots, and small wet umbrellas up and down the halls made the windows fog up. The weather didn't help the kids' moods, either. Mrs. Higgle had sent Jeremy Coats and Douglas McAllister to Mrs. Henshaw's office three times in three days. Indoor recess, indoor gym, and indoor science classes made it hard for kids not to get in trouble when they bumped into each other by mistake. Laura had seen very little of Meg and

Stevie since Mrs. Palmer set up what she called Bored Games for her class on rainy days at lunchtime.

"Uh, I don't think I can stand one more minute in the cafeteria after school," Shana said by Wednesday afternoon. She and Laura dragged their feet to the After-School Program.

"Sloppy Joes!" Laura said when they reached the cafeteria. "It was bad enough to have them at lunch, but the smell is worse now. Blech! I just hope we don't have to go to the gym and play 'What Time Is It, Mr. Fox' for the millionth time!"

"Since I don't get tutored today, what about if we ask Mrs. Whittaker, real nice, if we could stay and read in the cafeteria while the little kids go to the gym?" Shana suggested. "If you asked her, she might let us. You're such a good student and all."

"Tell that to Mrs. Higgle," Laura said. "Well, maybe I could try."

At 4:15, when the homework and tutoring time was up, Laura walked over to Mrs. Whittaker, who was lining up the younger After-Schoolers like ducks at the edge of a pond. "Mrs.

Whittaker? Mrs. Whittaker?" Laura asked, over all the chatter.

". . . and then if you all walk quietly to the gym, maybe we can play 'What Time Is It, Mr. Fox'," Mrs. Whittaker announced, as if she had just invented a great new game the children had never heard of.

"Again?" a few little ones cried. Even they were sick of it.

Mrs. Whittaker looked up just then and noticed Laura standing there, two heads taller than everyone else.

"What is it, Lauren?" Mrs. Whittaker asked.

Laura was going to have to yell out her message fast or she would find herself playing Mr. Fox any second. "Can Shana McCardle and I stay here in the reading corner and get ahead on our free reading instead of going to the gym?"

"You want to go to a meeting in the gym?" Mrs. Whittaker said back.

Laura began again, this time holding up a copy of *Nothing's Fair in Fifth Grade*. "Can Shana McCardle and I stay in the reading corner and do some of our free reading instead of going to the gym?"

Luckily Mrs. Whittaker was too distracted to say no. She had all she could do to keep Charles Rowan from tripping little Davey Macri. "Fine, fine, just stay in the reading corner," she said to Laura breathlessly.

Laura could hardly keep herself from jumping up and down and yelling, "Great! Great!" Instead, she made herself look very grown-up and responsible, which wasn't too hard. "Thank you."

"All riiight!" Shana said when Laura came back. "Maybe we don't always have to do everything with the little kids. Wouldn't that be great?"

"It'd be even greater if we could go to my house instead, but I'm stuck here for the rest of my life, I guess," Laura agreed. "Let's give ourselves five minutes to read, then we can talk."

The girls each pulled up a rectangle of carpet from the pile in the reading corner. Laura sat down Indian-style and opened her book while Shana stretched herself out and opened her latest copy of *Top Teens*.

"How do you think I'd look if I cut my hair like the singer in Lightning Strikes?" Shana asked Laura as she held open her magazine to show a picture of a rock band.

Laura looked up from her book. "You mean with short, short curly hair?" Laura couldn't picture Shana with anything but very straight spiky hair. In fact, she kind of liked it now that she knew Shana better.

"Maybe over the summer. You'd look good with it, don't you think? You would have to get a perm, though," Shana said as she studied Laura's long thick hair, which Laura usually wore with a plain hairband or in a French braid.

"I can't even stand getting a shampoo!" Laura protested.

"Are you done with your book?" Shana asked. "Maybe we can talk now that we did a little reading. I hate reading."

"Why?" Laura wanted to know.

"Reading books I mean. It takes too long. I wish we could do reports on rock stars or television shows or something," Shana sighed. "Then I'd be getting plusses instead of minuses. I never know what to pick from the reading list."

"I bet you'd like this," Laura said, holding up her book.

"*Nothing's Fair in Fifth Grade?*" Shana snorted. "Make that fourth grade, and I'll read it today!"

The two girls laughed, and their giggles echoed off the linoleum floor. Both girls leaned against the wall, glad to be free of Mrs. Whittaker. It was almost as good as being at home.

"My grades are getting a little better since Mr. Juliano started tutoring me," Shana confessed. "I got a check plus on the last math test."

"That's great," Laura said.

"I still hate writing, though. Mrs. Higgle just notices the mistakes and not what I was trying to say, you know what I mean?"

"Do I ever!" Laura groaned. "Thank goodness I have somebody to write to like Molly, who doesn't care if I indent or put three exclamation marks after sentences."

"That would make writing a whole lot easier." Shana paused and stared at the studs on her bright orange socks. "Would you ever show me one of Molly's letters or one of yours? What do you write about anyway?"

Laura thought for a long time. She had saved every one of Molly's letters in a special box at home. She shared them with Meg and Stevie, but she had never shown them to anyone else.

"I've got one here you can read if you want," Laura said shyly. She dug into her backpack and felt around the inside pocket for the thick envelope she had received just the Saturday before.

"Here's the last one she sent me," Laura said.

Shana's big hazel eyes looked wider than usual. "Are you sure? I mean, it's like reading somebody's diary or something. I was just wondering about your club and all, and what you think of to write about since you haven't seen each other for so long."

"Well, take a look," Laura said.

Shana pulled Molly's letter from the envelope slowly, as if it would crumble when she touched it. Laura busied herself at the bookshelves. Maybe she could find something good for Shana.

"Wow," Shana breathed when she finished reading the letter. "I can't believe you wrote to her about me. Molly sounds pretty nice." She paused. "And you're not bad, either!"

"Thanks," Laura said, pleased with Shana's half compliment. She had never seen Shana like this. Her whole face looked different. She had a dimple on her right cheek, which Laura had never noticed before, and her eyes were sparkling with happiness.

"Moving is hard, even if you're not the one that's leaving," Shana said next. "I thought you and Stevie and Meg never had any fights about anything. You always look . . . well, like sisters or something when I see you at lunch or walking down the halls."

"We are like sisters, I guess, but right now Stevie and Meg are like twins, and I'm the one who doesn't fit in," Laura confessed. "All because of stupid soccer."

Shana scrunched up her face just thinking about soccer. "Ugh, I hate sports."

"The only sport I like is ballet, even though it's not really a sport," Laura said. "But even that I don't much like anymore. I hate going alone, but my mother makes me because she never had ballet when she was little."

"You were so good in *The Magic Princess*. I don't know how you got up there and did all that, but you looked so graceful and into the music."

Laura remembered how much fun she and Meg had getting ready for the third-and-fourth-grade play. That had been hard, too, going to rehearsals, then coming home and doing homework. But it had been fun, too, another project the Friends 4-Ever had shared.

"Ballet's different now. I'm in a harder class." Laura sighed. "I just don't know if I want to keep going."

"You shouldn't give it up yet," Shana said. "Maybe it will get easier. Like my math, you know?"

"I guess," Laura said. She pulled at a thread on her pants and wound it around her finger until her finger turned red. "My mom makes me go just like she makes me go to the After-School Prison. So she'll have some place to stick me while she's at work."

Shana moved in a little closer to Laura. "Same here. Only instead of ballet, I have to get toootored."

Both girls sighed at the same time.

"Do you wish you were still in Florida?" Laura asked Shana.

"Sometimes," Shana confessed. "I'd probably be swimming right now. My mom used to let me come home right after school down there. See, I had this friend, Jill, and I could go to her apartment a lot, so my mom wouldn't worry about me while she was at work. Up here, it's different. I don't have anyplace to go to except here. . . ." Shana's voice trailed off.

"Do you write to that girl, Jill, or anything?" Laura wanted to know.

"We were going to," Shana said. "I sent her a birthday card. Maybe she'll send me one back."

Laura stared at her sneakers. An idea was just starting to shape in her mind. "Do you think you could ask your mom if you could come to my house tomorrow afternoon, maybe after tutoring?"

Shana tilted her head sideways a bit, and her parrot earrings swayed back and forth. "Why? What do you want to do?"

"It's a surprise. Just come over to my house after tutoring, and I'll tell you then," Laura said mischievously. "You'll need a note from home to give to Mrs. Higgle, and I'll bring one in, too. Do you think your mom will say it's okay?"

"I think so," Shana answered, pleased and puzzled at the same time. "I could maybe get ahead on my homework. That way she'd have to say yes."

"Great. Maybe I can even help you. Now what

does that article say about Lightning Strikes?" Laura asked.

"Well, here, let's read it together," Shana said excitedly. Both girls flipped onto their stomachs, spread out the magazine in front of them, and began reading the article. If Mrs. Higgle gave a test on *that* the next day, both girls would get check plusses.

SHANA'S GREAT IDEA

Laura got through lunch, two recesses, and a walk home without telling Meg and Stevie that Shana was coming to their club meeting. She was just going to do it and not have to listen to Meg and Stevie's wisecracks. They would just *have* to be nice to Shana.

Or else.

"What time are you coming over, Laura?" Meg asked when they reached the Ryders' house on the way home from school.

"Four-thirty."

"Can't you come earlier?" Meg asked. "We

have lots to do. We still haven't figured out how we can make more money at the tag sale. It's next week!"

"I know, I know. My mother's making me get my tag sale stuff organized today at the latest. It's the only day she's home," Laura grumbled. "Besides, I have to wait for . . ."

Meg and Stevie exchanged looks, the kind of looks they gave each other when they were suspicious about something.

"Well, you'll see at four-thirty," Laura said mysteriously as she went into the house.

"Hi, honey. Nothing from Molly," Mrs. Ryder called out when she saw Laura checking the mail. "Come have a muffin and some apple juice. I'm going to have a cup of tea."

Laura put down her backpack and made her way to the kitchen. "What's all this stuff, Mom?"

"Spring cleaning for the tag sale," her mother answered as she poured boiling water into a mug that said WORLD'S GREATEST MOM. "I put a couple of heavy garbage bags in your room. Maybe you can get started with your own things before your friend comes."

Laura sat down and peeled the foil cup from a blueberry muffin. She scrunched the foil into a ball and put it by her plate. That's when she noticed the ballet rehearsal schedule on the table.

Mrs. Ryder watched Laura. "I did the laundry today, Laura. I found this in your dance bag. I think today's a good time to talk about this, don't you?"

Suddenly Laura's bite of muffin felt dry in her throat. She took two long gulps of apple juice instead of answering her mother's question.

"I'm so glad Miss Humphrey set up more practice times. Now I can pick you up after the After-School Program and you can squeeze in a rehearsal then," Mrs. Ryder said. She circled a row of Mondays and Wednesdays, then held up the sheet. "How does this look?"

Laura didn't look up. She traced her finger around the border of the little yellow teacup her mother was going to sell.

"Are these days bad? We can't do Thursdays because of your meetings with Meg and Stevie. Fridays I know you're pretty eager for the weekend and won't want a rehearsal."

"I don't want to be in the recital this year," Laura finally managed to say. Her eyes were glittering with angry tears.

Mrs. Ryder's eyes opened wide as she leaned

in toward Laura. "Honey! You've been in the recital since you were four! I spoke to Miss Humphrey about the schedule myself and pointed out that so many of the girls have big school projects due around the same time. And what with so many working parents, it would be nice to have a more flexible schedule. It's perfect."

"It's not perfect!" Laura cried. "I wish I could quit ballet. I'm sick of schedules. I'm sick of school. And I'm sick of doing everything I hate all by myself!" Laura bit her lip.

After a very long stretch of silence, Laura began to wish her mother would say something instead of sitting there trying not to yell.

Finally her mother spoke up in a serious voice Laura dreaded. "I don't want to spoil your afternoon with this. Especially since you have a date with your friend from school. But I want you to think about this some more. Your ballet lessons are very expensive, and you can't just quit before you finish out the session."

Laura pushed back her chair and dropped the rest of her muffin into the garbage can. When she got to her room, she grabbed one of the big black plastic bags her mother had left there. Without any plan she tossed things into the bag willy-nilly. A mismatched slipper-sock went in, tangled on the foot of Laura's old Raggedy Ann doll. She stuffed in her Aunt Ev's bridesmaid's gown that Laura had worn for dress-up dozens of times. And in went the fake leopard vest, two of her mother's old purses, and some paperbacks she read when she was seven.

Laura looked over her bookcase. There, sitting right next to one of her favorite books, *Angelina Ballerina*, was Angelina herself. A stuffed version, of course. The white mouse, wearing a tutu, had an expression that Laura often used to have herself, the joy of dancing. Molly, Stevie, and Meg had given Angelina to Laura for her eighth birthday, and she could still remember how the girls hovered around when she removed the wrapping paper. None of the girls got stuffed animals anymore, but Angelina was different. Laura liked to hug Angelina right before going onstage. For good luck.

She didn't hug her now. Everything was bad luck lately, and the little white mouse couldn't help her feel any better. Laura put Angelina into the bag, along with the snowflake costume, and her dance bag. Then she took a yellow plastic tie and pulled it tight around the top of the black bag. She was done.

Laura heard the doorbell ring just as she was dragging her bag down the cellar stairs. She ran upstairs to the front door. Shana stood on the porch and looked a little bashful about coming in.

"Hi, Shana," Laura said, flushed and out of breath. "I'll be ready in a couple of minutes. Then we're going to Meg's."

"We are?" Shana asked. She looked around the Ryders' living room as if she didn't quite know where to stand.

"I'll tell you about it on the way over, okay? It'll be fun," Laura said, though she wasn't sure about that at all.

Mrs. Ryder came into the living room and coughed. Then she coughed again. Laura knew she should introduce her mother and Shana to each other, but her thoughts were zooming around in her head at about a hundred miles an hour.

"Um . . . um, this is my mom," Laura said finally without looking at her mother once.

"Hello, Shana," Mrs. Ryder said. "I already

know you a little from the Americana Festival last November and the holiday concert."

"Hi," Shana said quietly. "I'm . . . I'm sort of early, I guess. Mr. Juliano says I only have to get tutored for half an hour from now on. He said you and I could work on spelling and stuff together. If you want, I mean."

"Hey, that's great," Laura replied. "More time for us!" Maybe it wasn't such a bad-news day after all.

"I'm glad you two girls will have more time together," Mrs. Ryder said. "And I'm very glad you could come over this afternoon, Shana."

Laura wished her mom would stop being so nice. If she kept it up, Laura was going to have a hard time staying mad at her.

"We're going to Meg's," Laura said. She guided Shana to the front door.

"Have a good time," Mrs. Ryder called back. "Be back by six for dinner."

"Did you tell Meg and Stevie I was coming?" Shana asked as the girls walked down Double-tree Court.

"Well, not exactly," Laura confessed. Suddenly she was nervous about her brave plan. Now that she and Shana were actually going to a Friends 4-Ever meeting, Laura got worried about how everyone would get along. Was Stevie going to say something embarrassing about Shana's latest outfit? Would Meg act as if she had never seen Shana before?

"The houses are nice on this street," Shana said as the girls walked by yard after yard trimmed with tulips and daffodils. "On Church Street, it's mostly apartments and two-families, you know?"

"Do you live in an apartment?" Laura asked.

"Yeah, we almost got a house in Florida, but when my mom got a job up here, we got an apartment again. No jumping, no pets, and no loud music."

"Sounds like my house," Laura said.

"Is this it?" Shana asked when Laura slowed down in front of a pretty white house with a bright red door.

"Yup," Laura said. She took a deep breath. This was going to be some meeting.

"Come in, come in, girls," Mrs. Milano said when the girls came to the door. "I didn't know you had a new member," Mrs. Milano said, holding out her hand to Shana. "I'm Meg's mother."

"Hi," Shana said as she stared down at her neon pink-and-black sneakers.

"This is Shana . . . from school," Laura said.

"Well, just head upstairs. The girls are already there, probably discussing today's rules, if I know my daughter."

"C'mon. Up here," Laura said, coaxing Shana up the stairs. What a terrible idea this great idea now seemed.

Both girls stood in front of Meg's door. Laura felt silly giving the special Friends 4-Ever knock the way she usually did when she got to a meeting at Meg's or Stevie's, so she skipped it.

"I'm . . . I mean, we're here," she announced after one ordinary knock.

Stevie and Meg were sitting on the floor with their clipboards when Laura walked in with Shana. They looked up at exactly the same moment and blinked at the same time when they saw Laura wasn't alone. Then they gave each other an obvious what's-she-doing-here look.

"Hi," Laura said.

Nothing.

Laura coughed.

Nothing.

Now it was obvious she was in charge of the

talking. "I brought Shana," she announced.

Meg and Stevie seemed to be glued to the floor and didn't move an eyelash.

"Shana, you can sit here," Laura said, guiding her friend to the last empty corner of Meg's room.

"I guess you guys did some packing before I got here," Laura said.

Silence.

"I got some stuff ready, too," Laura said to Meg and Stevie. Then she turned to Shana and explained. "We're supposed to clean out our rooms and sell our things at the Crispin Landing Tag Sale we have every year. Then we're going to buy our own phones."

"We hope." Stevie finally broke the awful quiet.

"And if our parents let us," Meg added. She coughed when her voice cracked. "Do you have your own phone already, Shana?"

"No. It's . . . it's just my mom and me, and we don't know that many people, so we just have one phone," Shana said quietly.

"Last year we only made eight dollars, so we probably won't get phones, either," Stevie grumbled. "I have to share ours with my brothers." She looked up to see if Shana was going to say anything about Mike, but Shana didn't seem to realize right then and there that Mike Ames and Stevie Ames were even related.

"Eight dollars won't buy a wire on a phone," Meg complained. "Unless we can think of some other way to make money at the tag sale."

Shana wriggled around as if she were uncomfortable or wanted to say something she wasn't sure she should say.

"What do you think, Shana?" Laura asked. Maybe there was some way she could get her into the plans.

"Well," Shana began, "when I was in Florida, my mom and I went to lots of tag sales to buy furniture and things we needed for our apartment. Down there, in some of the places, kids sell things to eat and — "

"We did that last year," Meg interrupted, "but we ate half of what we made."

"And spilled the rest!" Stevie chimed in, remembering the big fruit punch stain on the driveway.

"It was just an idea," Shana mumbled. She sank back against the wall.

"Shana didn't know we tried that already,

guys," Laura said. She was getting annoyed. Why did Meg and Stevie have to be such know-it-alls anyway? "Let's try to think of something else."

Except for the regular snapping of Stevie's gum, the room was quiet again.

"There sort of is something else," Shana began again.

Stevie and Meg exchanged looks.

"You could do games for kids who come around with their parents, and charge them money," Shana suggested.

"Like what kind of games?" Meg asked, examining a freckle on her arm without even looking up.

"Like Double Dare stuff. You know, make up silly games and charge people to be in them. My friend, Jill Corey, and I went to a street fair in her neighborhood where they did games like that, and we had a lot of fun. We spent our money on that instead of buying more junk at the tag sale tables."

Meg began doodling on her clipboard. Laura couldn't tell if she and Stevie thought this was the dumbest idea ever or what.

"What kind of games?" Stevie asked.

"Like on TV. You know, Jell-O races or trying to throw fish over somebody's head into a bucket. They gave us old T-shirts and raincoats to wear so we wouldn't get too disgusting!" Shana said with a big smile. "Jill and I . . . well, we had lots of fun that day! Even though we needed showers when we got home!"

"Do you ever talk to her? Your friend, I mean?" Meg wanted to know. "I mean, how do you get it organized, and what do you charge, and . . . wait, let me get a pencil."

Stevie leaned over and whispered to Shana, "Meg's not really happy unless she has a list. Watch."

Shana smiled. "I haven't talked to Jill since we moved. We were going to write, but I'm not the greatest writer."

"Me, neither," Stevie announced, snapping her cinnamon gum at the very thought. "I can't believe I belong to a club where all we do is write letters!"

"Stevie! Come on, admit it. You like getting Molly's letters even more than Laura and I do," Meg pointed out. "You just said today how you reread a letter Molly sent you last September!"

Stevie cocked her head sideways as if she

knew something so obvious that it was practically written on her forehead. "I never said I didn't like *reading* Molly's letters, I just don't like *writing* them. There's a difference."

"Well, I don't know what the difference is," said Meg.

Laura looked at Shana and explained. "Meg's already on her second box of stationery and — "

" — and Stevie has enough left over to wallpaper my room!" Meg said as she rolled her eyes. "Well, how would you like *not* to write a letter today, Stevie?"

"Anything, I'll do anything," Stevie said. "I'll clean your room. I'll paint your house. I'll do your homework. No. Forget the last part."

"Shana, do you have the address of your friend, Jill?" Meg asked.

Shana finally looked happy to be there and gave a little jiggle of her loopy earrings. "I have it at home."

"Why don't we write a letter to her and ask if she could help us plan something for our tag sale? Games and things?" All of a sudden Meg was acting as if it were all her idea to ask Shana to the meeting.

Shana looked at Laura, and Laura gave her a

big silvery smile, braces and all.

"Here, you can use my clipboard," Stevie said.

"And my stationery. It's got cute kittens on it," Meg said as she offered Shana several sheets of paper. "Laura can write to Molly while we think of things to ask your friend. Ask her what we need to get ahead of time, what the games were, what to charge. Here, I'll make a list."

"Meg needs a list just to get out of bed in the morning," Stevie joked.

Laura sat down at Meg's desk and began her own letter. She had so much to tell to Molly.

Dear Molly,

You were right again! I invited Shana to our meeting, and she's HERE!!! At first Meg and Stevie acted funny (not funny funny the way Stevie usually does) but looking at each other funny, like I walked in with an alien or something.

But then, you won't believe this. Shana

gave us the greatest idea for the tag sale —
to run games like Double Dare for the kids
who come with their parents, and charge
them money.

We're still going to sell our stuff, but we
need to make more money if we want to get
phones (we haven't told our parents yet) and
Shana's idea is the greatest. What do you
think?

You're the greatest, too, for helping me
figure out how to have a new friend and still
have my old friends. But even if I meet ten
Shanas, you'll still be the friend I think about
the most.

2 Sweet 2 B 4-gotten,

Laura

ALMOST-PERFECT PLANS

Laura sat on the edge of her chair. Five more clicks of the second hand and she was free.

"Okay, everyone, remember, tomorrow is your spelling review. It counts one third of your grade," Mrs. Higgle announced. "One third!"

"One third! One third!" Laura and Shana mimicked when they were safely out in the hall after the last bell.

"C'mon," Shana said, pulling Laura down the hall toward the cafeteria. "Today I can't wait to go to After-School Prison. I've got lots to tell you about what Jill said about the tag sale."

"Hey, guys! Wait up!" Shana and Laura heard over the buzz of voices in the hall.

Laura felt a hand pull on her French braid. The puller was Stevie. "Geez, you two. You'd think they were giving away free candy in the After-School Program the way you were racing down the hall."

"I got a letter from Jill," Shana announced excitedly.

"Well, where is it?" Meg demanded.

Shana sighed. "You won't believe this, but I can't find it. I thought I put it someplace I'd remember, but I forgot where."

"You forgot?" Meg groaned in disbelief. "I guess we'll have to have an emergency meeting so we can look for it."

"We don't need an emergency meeting, Meg," Laura began. "Shana and I can talk about what Jill said during After-School Prison. Besides, Shana's got her own ideas, too."

Meg didn't look so sure of this. "Don't you think we ought to have a meeting?" she whined to nobody in particular.

"No, we don't," Stevie piped up. "Remember? We have a game? With Springhurst? So just forget about any emergency meetings and put your clipboard away. Laura and Shana can tell us what we have to do."

"Oh, all right," Meg muttered. She didn't like the idea of someone else, even Laura, getting a head start on organizing the tag sale. "Can you at least tell me a *little* about what Jill said?"

"No, she can't, Meg," Stevie broke in. "Now come on! We've got to get to Pierson Park. Maybe Mr. Harding will let *you* coach the game."

"Don't worry, Meg," Shana said. "I already started on a list and made some drawings of where we can set up the games. Jill told me what to do, so don't worry about anything."

Meg looked doubtful. Nobody could organize a club or an event or even a trip to the mailbox like she could. "Okay, but I *need* that letter before our meeting next Thursday."

"See you guys," Stevie said, dodging and passing between the kids waiting in the bus area. She followed an imaginary soccer ball through the crowd and could practically hear the coach urging her on to a goal.

"I'd better go, or I'll never catch her," Meg complained.

" 'Bye, Meg. Don't worry," Laura said, turning Meg around and pointing her toward the door. "We'll just do a rough draft of a list, like in Writing Workshop. You can do the final."

"Okay." Meg hugged Laura and smiled at Shana before running off to catch Stevie.

"I always feel like I should salute Meg," Shana said as she and Laura went into the cafeteria toward their own study table.

"I know," Laura said, thinking about Meg. "I wouldn't do half the things I do if it weren't for Meg. She's always got lots of plans."

"And jobs," Shana laughed.

The girls got out their spelling lists and quizzed each other on their words as fast as they could so they could talk about something important: Jill Corey's letter.

"Zipper. Same ending as dipper, flipper," Laura said to Shana.

"Z - I - P - P - E - R," Shana answered. "Those little hints you always give me help a lot. Mrs. Higgle said I could go to the harder list after this one." Shana looked pleased and proud of herself.

"You'll be sorreee," Laura said. "Now tell me what Jill said."

The girls leaned in toward each other and shut out the noisy sounds of the other kids in the cafeteria.

"I'm sorry about forgetting the letter, Laura. Meg looked kind of mad," Shana said. "Anyway, I know it by heart, so it doesn't matter."

"Meg's always like that. She likes to save everything and look at it a hundred times," Laura said, trying to make Shana feel better. "She thinks it makes our meetings more official. You know, like our club has important documents."

"I'll remember that next time," Shana said. "Anyway, Jill said we should have a shaving cream slide that kids go down."

"Yeeww!" Laura said at the very thought of getting squishy shaving cream all over herself. "What else?"

"Jell-O relay races. Fish-throwing into a bucket," Shana said. "And I had another great idea. Set up the tent you told me about, but turn it into a haunted house where kids hear creepy stories and feel disgusting things while they're blindfolded. Peeled grapes for eyeballs, oily spaghetti for brains."

Laura shivered. "Oooo, that's a great idea,"

she said. Out of all the girls, Laura was the one who still got really tingly and scared whenever Meg or Stevie told spooky stories. Her mother was forever telling her not to listen, but Laura just couldn't help it.

"I'm really glad Meg said to write to Jill," Shana said. "I already wrote back, and we're going to keep writing. As long as she doesn't give me C-minuses on my writing like you-know-who."

"I know what you mean," Laura sighed. "Well, Meg will kill us if we don't get a list started or some plans down on paper."

"I already started," Shana said proudly, reaching for her clipboard. "See, I made drawings of where to set up each game. The Water Balloon Throw near the garage and the Fish Throw near the big maple tree."

Laura looked at Shana's little map and the stick figures of each of the four girls supervising various tables, booths, and games. That part was going to be so much fun.

Then Laura felt a tiny flip-flop. Someone else would be buying Angelina and her ballet things at the White Elephant Table. Everything was still squashed at the bottom of the black garbage bag, which was now sitting in a garage on Half Moon Lane along with a lot of old lamps, musty curtains, and used board games.

"What's the matter, Laura? Don't you like the plans?" Shana asked.

"I do, I do," Laura insisted, but she was too embarrassed to tell Shana that she was all upset about a stuffed animal. She decided to tell her about something else that was starting to bother her. "Now that it's getting closer, I keep wondering if my parents are cleaning out our house so we can get a bigger one. I know this is dumb, but my dad is selling our lawn mower."

Shana tilted her head and looked confused. "Why should that get you upset?"

"What if my dad needs a bigger lawn mower because we're getting a bigger yard? You know, now that my mom makes more money? Did your mother start getting rid of things before she told you about moving to Rhode Island?"

Shana started laughing. "My mom never gets rid of anything! You know what else? She says not to worry about things that might not happen. Then when they happen, she says not to worry because there's nothing you can do about it. So it all works out."

Now it was Laura's turn to laugh. "My parents *love* to worry about everything! If I have to stay with somebody while they're out, they show where all the fire exits are and what to do if the lights go out! Not to mention that I have to wear a dumb helmet when I'm bike riding just in case I go over a curb and crack my head open like a girl did who my mother heard about. Honestly," Laura sighed. "All they do is worry about stuff."

"I bet that's why they put you in the After-School Program. In case there was a hurricane and they were at work," Shana laughed.

"Or a tornado," Laura added.

"Or a flood," Shana said.

"Or a tree fell on the house."

"Or a plane fell out of the sky."

When the girls ran out of disasters to laugh about, Shana went back to her clipboard, and Laura began a letter to Molly:

Dear Molly,

Your last letter was a big help. Something was (is) bothering me, more than Meg and Stevie playing soccer. I'm mad at my mom and I can't stop! I keep thinking she makes me do things so she can just go have a good time at her job.

You won't believe what I did. I forgot (on purpose) to sign up for the ballet recital. I didn't tell you 'cause I know you wish you could be here dancing, too. I even told my mom I want to quit dance, but she says I have to go. Worst, worst of all, we had a HUGE fight, and I threw out my ballet stuff and put it in the tag sale bag. (Yes, even Angelina.) Now I feel so awful I don't know what to do. (The White Elephant Sale is going to be at Mrs. Hansen's, at your old house. Her grandchildren are going to run the toy table while we run the games at

Meg's. *Angelina's probably worth a hundred dollars!)*

You know when you don't want to think about something (like when I was about to get braces or you were about to move) and no matter what you do, that's all you think about? Well, I saw my dad's lawn mower in the garage with a price tag for the sale and a yellow teacup of my mom's with a sticker for the sale, and now I keep worrying that my mom got this job so we can get a bigger house. And I want to stay where we are!

Am I just being a worrywart for nothing? Please write back right away.

Your Friend 4 Ever,

Laura

When Laura was done, her fingers ached from gripping her pencil so hard. She folded the letter quickly and stuffed it into the envelope.

"Hey, that looks longer than the book report I wrote," Shana said when she noticed the fat envelope Laura was addressing. "Did you tell Molly all about our plans?"

"Only some of them," Laura said quietly.

SUPER SATURDAY

"Stevie Ames's wake-up service!"

It was only seven in the morning, but Laura heard Stevie's voice followed by the Friends 4-Ever knock. She pulled a blanket over her head to block out the noise and the sunlight squeezing through the shutters.

"Hey, Laura, wake up, wake up!" The door burst open, and Stevie stood there grinning and wide awake, wearing a bright yellow Crispin Landing T-shirt and a pair of cut-off jeans. "Meg sent me over to get you going. We have to set up. Half the neighborhood's out there already."

Laura yawned and didn't even have the energy to push strands of her long brown hair from her still-sleepy eyes. "Go away," she groaned.

Stevie decided that what Laura meant by "Go away" was "Pull off the cover," so that's just what she did.

"Stevie! What are you doing?" Laura cried, mad as a bee.

"Today's the day we get rich, Laura! Don't you want to get started?" Stevie cried. She hopped onto Laura's bed and started bouncing. "Come on! Let's go!"

"I guess I'll get dressed," Laura said. She tried to stick a leg out from under the covers but pulled it right back under.

"We got the doughnut holes already," Stevie told her friend. "Mr. Milano went to Bella's and got four boxes full. We're going to make a bundle. After we pay him back, of course."

"Don't mention food," Laura said grumpily. Just the thought of doughnut holes made her morning stomach do backflips.

"Coconut, cinnamon, glazed. Mmm, I have some right here, Laura." Stevie held up a small bag filled with doughnut holes.

"Ugh. Are you going to eat more than we sell

this year, too?" Laura asked in a croaky voice.

"Just these. I promise," Stevie said with a big grin. Then she popped a doughnut hole into her mouth as Laura slowly got dressed in the same T-shirt and cut-offs that Stevie was wearing.

Mrs. Ryder stuck her head in the door. "Good. You're up, Laura. Dad and I will be out front all day in case you need us."

"She won't," Stevie piped up. "We're going to be at Meg's all day. Getting rich!"

Mrs. Ryder smiled at Stevie and Laura, but only Stevie smiled back. "Are you feeling okay, Laura? You look a bit peaky."

"It's too early," Laura grumbled.

"Honestly, Jim, I don't know what's gotten into Laura lately," she heard her mother say quietly to her father. Not quietly enough.

Stevie looked at Laura for a long time. "What has gotten into you, Laura? A bug? A tack? My mom's always saying something's gotten into me. It makes me feel like I swallowed something by mistake."

Laura was still too sleepy to laugh. Everybody was just so bright and wide awake this morning, she could hardly stand it.

"C'mon Laura. Meg's going to fine us if we

don't get to her house soon," Stevie urged. She tried to pull Laura's arm, but Laura pulled it back.

"Hey, don't spend it all in one place," Mr. Ryder said when the two girls came outside where he was dusting off their old lawn mower. "How much do you think I could get for this old clunker, girls?"

Stevie studied the clouds for a second. "Maybe you could *give* somebody five dollars to take it away!"

Laura walked slowly ahead to Doubletree Court while Stevie did her usual running, hopping, and zigzagging routine all the way to Meg's.

"We're here," Stevie cried when they got to the Milanos' house. "Anybody got water balloons?" Stevie stuck her head under the basketball hoop on the garage for the Water Balloon Throw. Then she posed inside a huge cardboard gorilla cutout that Mr. Milano had painted. The girls were planning to charge a dollar for each instant photo of anyone who wanted a picture taken looking like a gorilla.

"Laura, Stevie, look what we put up!" Meg cried. She pointed to a red plastic bucket nailed to the maple tree. "It's to catch the sardines during the Fish Throw."

"How about a doughnut-hole throwing contest?" Stevie called out from the food table, where thermoses of coffee and jugs of lemonade and the vanishing doughnut holes were displayed.

"Stevie!" Meg screamed. "Don't you think of anything but food?"

Laura watched all this going on and wished she were back in bed. She just wasn't quite ready for the day now that it was here and hoped no one would notice.

"Hey, there's Shana. I guess that's her mom with her," Meg announced as an old tan car drove up the road.

"Help!" Shana cried out. "Can somebody get some of this?"

The other three girls could barely see Shana's face, she was so hidden by a cardboard box and two heavy bags.

"Hello, I'm Shana's mother, Lorraine Mc-Cardle," a tall black-haired woman said to Mr. and Mrs. Milano. She gave the girls a big smile as Shana joined them.

"Mom, this is Stevie, Meg, and Laura," Shana

said. The girls leaned into each other as if they were a team.

"Hi," they said shyly all at the same time. They tried not to stare, but they had never seen a grown-up they knew wear spiky hair and sparkly sneakers.

"Hi. We've got a good day for this, don't you think?" Meg's mother said. "Would you like some coffee?"

"Would you like someone to throw a wet fish at you, Mom?" Shana chimed in.

"I have a feeling I know whose idea that was," Mrs. McCardle said. "Shana and her friend Jill tagged along with me at many tag sales in Florida when we moved there. In one neighborhood, the children made money with silly games they copied from television."

"Double Dare!" the girls all cried out together.

"Whatever," Mrs. McCardle said. "I think there are some great bargains at these things. Look at this. I picked it up for a quarter. At your house, Laura." With a big smile, Mrs. McCardle pulled out an orange-and-brown pitcher Laura's mother had tried to sell three years in a row.

"It's lovely," Mrs. Milano said. "Just needs a few wildflowers."

"I'm going to do some more bargain-hunting," Mrs. McCardle said. "I'll be back for you at five, Shana."

" 'Bye, Mom," Shana answered, then turned to inspect the work the girls had done.

By this time, cars were driving slowly up Doubletree Court, and parking places were going fast. The girls positioned themselves by the games, but all the early birds were grown-ups.

"Hot coffee. Get your hot coffee!" Stevie cried out as she scampered over to the food table. "C'mon, guys. I don't think those people look like they're going to want to have a gorilla picture taken."

"Or throw fish into the bucket," Meg sighed. "I guess we'll have to wait 'til later when the families come with their kids."

"And their allowances!" Stevie cackled.

"I know. Even in Florida, it's always older people who come first," Shana said.

"Looking for old plates," Meg added.

Sure enough, just across the street at the Barbellas', several elderly people were examining old glasses and cracked bowls.

The girls were restless and started doing cart-wheels in between pouring coffee and juice for a few people who had straggled over. Laura sat under Meg's tree and started wondering if Mrs. Hansen had any customers yet.

"How much have you girls made?" Mr. Milano asked when he and Meg's mother came out to check on how the girls were doing.

"A dollar ten," Stevie said in disgust.

"Well, hang in there, girls. Don't forget, Mrs. Hansen has your things. Maybe she's made some big sales there," Mrs. Milano said.

"Let's hope she got rid of that big ugly yellow rabbit," Mr. Milano added.

"Daddy!" Meg cried. "I had him practically my whole life!"

"And he looks it, too," Meg's father grumbled.

"Shana, can I bring your bags to Mrs. Hansen's? Nothing's happening here yet," Laura said.

"Sure, but come right back. Usually kids start coming after the cartoons are over."

"I'll be back in ten minutes."

"Bring back some little kids," Stevie yelled out. "With lots of money!"

Laura walked down the street and when she rounded the corner, she walked by her own house.

"Where you headed, Laura?" her father called out when she passed their house. The lawn mower was still leaning against the pine tree.

"Just have to drop these off at the White Elephant Table at Mrs. Hansen's," Laura answered back.

There were cars backed up on Half Moon Lane and people swarming everywhere. Laura saw two kids go by with a rusty scooter that had belonged to Greg Egan before he outgrew it. Laura watched every child there to see if anyone was walking off with a white-and-silver tutu or a purple dance bag. Or a mouse who loved dancing.

Mrs. Hansen, who was wonderful at sewing things, had made a large white stuffed elephant and hung it from a branch of the dogwood tree in front of her house. There were several older women gathered around the tree looking at Mrs. Hansen's handmade afghans.

"Hello, Laura," Mrs. Hansen said when she noticed Laura at the edge of the crowd. "The children's table is on the other side of the driveway. Why don't you go take a look? My grand-children have sold quite a few things already."

Laura felt a little sick the closer she got to the toy table.

"Hi, Laura," Jenny Hansen said, looking very professional as she counted out money from an old cigar box. "Here's some of your stuff."

Laura looked at the far end of the table where Jenny pointed. "Is this everything?"

"I'm not sure," Jenny answered. "My sister sold some things before, but then she had to leave. She left this envelope with your name on it."

"Thanks," Laura said, reaching for the enve-lope. "Here are some more toys to sell for our club. I'll put them under the table until there's more space."

The white envelope was heavy. Laura opened it up and saw several one-dollar bills and a lot of change. Now she knew for sure. Some other person had bought all her things. Just a few old paperbacks and records were left on her corner of the table.

Mrs. Hansen walked over to Laura. "What is it, dear? Are you disappointed about the money? You know some of these people drive a hard bargain. Why, I had to sell my Morning Star quilt for half of what I wanted! I just won't be able to take it all if I have to move into an apartment."

Mrs. Hansen's soft blue eyes looked so sad and far away that Laura forgot all about her own hollow feelings for a minute. She just wanted to go sit in Mrs. Hansen's kitchen and listen to her talk about her husband and the nice trips they made before he died. Laura knew they would both feel better if they were inside Molly's old house, which always smelled like lilacs and apples now that Mrs. Hansen lived there. Some awful bargain hunter had bought one of her beautiful quilts and probably drove off with Angelina besides!

"You didn't sell your bells, did you?" Laura said softly.

"No, not those. I collected those bells one by one when Mr. Hansen was alive. I'll leave them to my grandchildren someday. There are some things you should always keep," Mrs. Hansen said, squeezing Laura's hand. "Now that big yellow rabbit over there certainly isn't one of them, is it?" Mrs. Hansen added with a nod toward Meg's huge old and quite ugly stuffed rabbit.

"Would you take a dollar for this?" an older man said to Mrs. Hansen when she got back to her table.

"Well, I don't know about that, you see . . ." Mrs. Hansen spoke so softly, Laura could no longer hear her.

Laura walked slowly down Half Moon Lane. If only she'd talked to Mrs. Hansen about the bells before, she would never have sold Angelina. But now it was too late.

When Laura turned onto Crispin Landing Road, she saw groups of people all over her front lawn. Her mother was standing by a rack of Laura's outgrown clothes, and her dad was trying to convince yet another customer about what a fine lawn mower he had to sell. A bargain.

"Laura, why aren't you down at the games?" her mother shouted before crossing the road to meet her. "What is it?"

Laura swallowed hard. "Nothing. I was just looking around. I'm going back to Meg's now." She noticed a red plaid dress draped over her mother's arm. "What's that?"

Her mother sighed. "Don't you remember? You wore this on the first day of kindergarten.

Someone offered me five dollars for it and before I realized what I was saying, I told her it was sold! I just couldn't bear to sell it."

"How come?" Laura said, looking at the dress with its deep ruffle and big tie in the back. She barely remembered it and certainly couldn't imagine herself wearing such a dress.

"It just made me realize what a long time ago kindergarten was, that's all. And now here you are in fourth grade, all grown up. That was five years ago. I was even thinking that maybe you really are too old to have to stay at school."

"Really?" Laura looked up at her mother hopefully.

"Well, not every day anyway. But Shana's mother was one of my first customers today. She bought that pitcher I've been trying to sell. I don't know if I was so happy about that or what, but we got to talking and we might let you girls come here one afternoon and go to her apartment another day. What with my day off on Thursdays, you'd only have to go to the After-School Program two days a week. I still have to discuss it with your father, of course, but — "

"Can I? I mean, can we, Mom? I promise I'll get my homework done and not watch too much television and not answer the door without checking first. Please, please, can I?" Laura pleaded.

"We'll see," Mrs. Ryder answered. But she was smiling.

"Well, have you made your fortune?" Mr. Ryder said when he walked over to Laura and her mother. "I don't think this will add to the down payment much, Lynn."

Mrs. Ryder poked her husband in the ribs. "I thought we were going to tell Laura later," she whispered.

"Tell me what?" Laura's voice cracked. Were they going to ruin the good news about coming home in the afternoons with some other, terrible news?

Her parents were grinning, and her dad put his right arm around Laura and his left arm around Mrs. Ryder. "We're buying our house," he announced.

"Which house?" Laura cried.

"The one we live in, silly," Mrs. Ryder said. "The Ackerlys decided they like Florida so much, they're going to stay down there. They gave us a good price and with my job and all, I think we can swing it."

"This house? This house?" Laura repeated.

"Now don't go telling me your room is too small," Mrs. Ryder said, "because we're about to own it!"

"Oh, mom, I love my room. Even though it is too small," Laura added with a big grin. "I was getting worried lately that we were going to move someplace else. Especially when I saw Daddy trying to sell our lawn mower."

Mrs. Ryder sighed. "That thing! Dad just wants to get a power mower, that's all. He can do a better job on the yard once we own the house." Mrs. Ryder hugged Laura. "You shouldn't worry about things that might not happen. Why didn't you tell us about this?"

"I don't know. Everything else was going wrong, I guess I thought other bad things might happen. Like leaving this house."

"The only bad thing that's going to happen is fixing up this place," Mr. Ryder broke in. "And having to mow the lawn with that darn thing," he added, pointing to the unsold mower.

"Now you better scoot along, Laura, or you won't make very much today," Mrs. Ryder said. "I'll come down later to see how you girls made out."

Meg's yard was swarming with little kids when Laura got back. Meghan Basher's head was sticking out of the gorilla picture, dimples and all.

"Yuck!" Scotty Toth screamed as his little brother, Matthew, tried to pitch sardines over his head into the bucket on the tree. "Can't you aim a little better?" Scott kept saying as the fish slithered down his neck.

"Laura! Laura! Where were you?" Meg shouted. She was busy supervising the messy Jell-O relay races. "We need somebody to collect quarters from the kids when they line up for the games."

"All right! All right! I'm here," Laura said, reaching for the fishing box the girls were using as a money box.

"Where did you go?" Shana asked when she came out of the orange tent the girls had set up as a haunted house. Shana had found a tall, pointed witches' hat, which went perfectly with yet another of her almost all-black outfits. "I need somebody to tie bandannas on the little kids and line them up for the haunted house. I've got the bowl of peeled grapes and the oily spaghetti already," she whispered so some of

117

the younger children wouldn't hear.

Laura grabbed a folding chair and set it up in the middle of the lawn. She attached the big sign that said: HAUNTED HOUSE! SLIMY GAMES, AND MORE, $.25 A TURN.

"Here's my twenty-five cents," little Willie Mosa said. "I know it's just peeled grapes like we had at Halloween."

"No it's not," Laura said, handing Willie a handmade ticket. "We got them right from the Old Dutch Graveyard."

"Yeah, yeah," Willie said as he turned around and Laura tied the bandanna around his eyes and led him into the tent.

"Come into my haunted house," Shana's cackly voice called from inside.

Laura spent the morning and the afternoon making more tickets, tying on more bandannas, and filling more water balloons while Meg, Stevie, and Shana ran the games.

By four-thirty, the Milanos' ivy and daffodils were drooping from all the children who had walked or run over them to get to the games. The Jell-O cubes were long melted. Word was out among the neighborhood children that the slimy brain they had paid so many quarters to touch was nothing more than a big round lump of cold, oily spaghetti.

"Twelve dollars," Stevie groaned. "All that for just twelve dollars. We'll never get our phones now!"

"Not real ones," Shana said. "That's for sure."

"Who's going to give Meg the bad news?" Shana asked.

Shana, Stevie, and Laura all looked down the street toward Meg, who was coming back from Mrs. Hansen's with the money from the toy table.

"She's walking kind of slow," Laura said.

When Meg got back to her yard her face was all red. "Fifty cents! They sold my yellow rabbit for fifty cents! I don't believe it!"

"How much for all our other stuff?" Stevie wanted to know. "I've got twelve dollars here. Maybe with what we got from the stuff Mrs. Hansen sold for us we can — "

"Forget it, Stevie. All we made was six dollars and twenty-one cents."

"Plus this," Laura said, pulling her money out of her pocket. "Mrs. Hansen's granddaughter sold my Angelina doll and some of my other ballet stuff."

Shana, Meg, and Stevie looked at each other as if they had a big secret. "That's not from your ballet stuff, Laura, it must be from your books and your other toys."

"What do you mean?"

"Wait," Shana said. She ran into the tent and came out with a black garbage bag. "Here."

Laura was puzzled. She opened the top of the bag and looked inside. There was her Snowflake tutu inside her dance bag. And underneath that was . . . "Angelina!" Laura cradled the dancing mouse in her arms. "Where did you guys get her? I put her in with my other stuff and my dad brought it to Mrs. Hansen's to sell."

"And we got it back when we found out from Molly what you did!" Stevie said proudly. "I mean, I don't know a ballet step from a touchdown, but when Molly found out about how you wanted to quit ballet and you were going to sell your ballet junk, she told us to get it back."

"I've got a letter from her in my house. Wait, I'll go get it," Meg said as she ran into her house.

When Meg came out, she handed Laura an envelope. "Here, read it."

Dear Meg,

This is TOP SECRET! even though we're not supposed to have any secrets in our club. I just got a letter from Laura saying how miserable she is 'cause you guys go running off and do your stuff and forget about what she likes. Like ballet. Like her new friend Shana. Anyway, she got so upset about everybody telling her to do this or do that (like the After-School Program or going to soccer, when you know she's a dancer) she got mixed up about what to do and went off and sold her ballet stuff and didn't sign up for the recital.

Here's what you've got to do. No matter what, get her stuff back before somebody buys it. Then tell her how all of us almost quit Mrs. Perlmutter's art classes at first because we had to be so grown-up instead of mooshing paints and clay like we used to when we were *little. Remember how our parents made us keep going? Then we got prizes in the library art show. There's always a hard part before it gets fun again. Tell her that.*

As for you and Stevie, instead of telling me about how to get back at the Terrible Three, you two should listen to Laura. Anybody she picks for a friend is going to be great 'cause she's so great. Got it?

Your Friend 4-Ever,

Molly

"Don't read that last paragraph," Meg and Stevie said at the same time, snatching the letter from Laura's hand.

"As if we could be *anything* like The Terrible Three, who are so mean to Molly," Meg sniffed.

"Looks like you're going to be needing that tutu thing again," Stevie said to Laura. "Maybe you'll get to be a raindrop instead of a snowflake this time."

"I don't think so." Laura spun in a pirouette. "The theme this year is 'Nocturne.'"

The girls all made puzzled crinkly faces.

"You'll see. It's going to be very dreamy and beautiful." Laura raised her arms and glided across the lawn, her shadow dancing right behind her.

Three other long skinny shadows joined Laura's, and they all danced until the sun set.

What happens when Meg goes to Kansas and discovers a new Molly? Read Friends 4-Ever #4, REMEMBER ME, WHEN THIS YOU SEE.